MURDER AND CONDOMONIUM

Thank you
and Enjoy —
Dick.

RICHARD V. BARRY

Winterlight Books

Shelbyville, KY USA

Murder and Condomonium
by Richard V. Barry

First Printing – September 2014
ISBN: 978-1-60047-988-5

Printed in the U.S.A.

0   1   2   3   4   5   6   7   8   9   10   11

BOOKS BY RICHARD V. BARRY

Short Stories

CROSSCURRENTS: Stories of People in Conflict
PERSONAL WARS
INFINITE GESTURES

Novels

AN INCONVENIENT DEATH
QUALITIES OF MERCY
IN EVIL'S VORTEX

Novella

History of the Smiling Young Lord

Non-Fiction

Misadventures in Europe
Experiencing Woodland Pond

1

The day that Nick Dalton dreaded was upon him: the Annual Meeting of the Marsden Grove Senior Condominium Association. When all the cranks, whiners and malcontents came crashing together in a dystopian carnival of inflated egos, enraged outbursts, long-winded harangues and simmering feuds.

On days like this, with all the condo owners assembled, it made Nick feel that there must have been some secret advertisements placed in arcane journals that attracted blowhards, dithering twits and those with borderline personality disorders to see Marsden Grove as the perfect setting for demonstrating rude, eccentric and outrageous behavior. Granted, there were many attractive, affable and sane seniors enjoying their retirement years in the pastoral setting of Marsden Grove, but, Nick reflected, their voices were usually drowned out at meetings like this by all the clamoring and bellowing of the fringe group.

On this blazing hot August morning, Nick sat behind the long table reserved for the Board of Managers, facing the audience. With mounting unease he surveyed the early arrivals as they took their seats on the folding chairs under a portable canvas top, set up on the lawn between the main parking area and the swimming pool pavilion. Frowns visible, eyes glaring, lips pursed, they had all the hallmarks of a lynch mob. Only a few smiling faces and pleasant exchanges relieved this dour picture.

At moments like these Nick often reflected on how the hell, at sixty-six, he had ever wound up at Marsden Grove. Then he'd flash back to three years ago when, in the course of five months, he had taken early retirement and lost his wife to cancer. Shadows and echoes of his beloved Judy haunted every room of the house they had shared for twenty-seven years, and he wanted out.

Marsden Grove, a gated condo community of attached townhouses, with twenty-four-hour security, was restricted to seniors sixty-two and older. Set next to a verdant golf course which, as an ardent golfer, Nick loved, and bordering a hundred-acre preserve, which, as an ardent hiker, Nick also loved, the community was not far from the south shore of Long Island with its roiling surf and wide, gleaming beaches, offering still another attraction to Nick who enjoyed surf casting. Since Marsden Grove was only a short distance from his present community, Nick felt he could easily maintain all his old friendships.

Acting impulsively, he made two quick visits to this three-year-old community and read the glossy brochure about the serene lifestyle of its residents. On his third visit he selected a two-bedroom, two-and-one-half-bath townhouse overlooking the sixth hole of the golf course and closed the deal. At sixty-four, he was only two years over the required age for residency. He gave his own house to his only child Tom and Tom's wife Vera, as they were still struggling in their early thirties for a firm financial footing. He left them most of the furniture since that evoked memories, too Taking only a few possessions and his beloved four-year-old chocolate lab Charley, Nick moved on to a new life. Only after he was a full-time resident did he realize what he had bought into.

Marsden Grove seemed to be a magnet for every kook and curmudgeon this side of the Hudson. Interspersed among these full-blown eccentrics were some very nice seniors.

Whenever Nick thought about the Marsden Grove population, he remembered something his wife, a high school art teacher, had said to him about fifteen percent of her students demanding eighty-five percent of her time. This inappropriate absorption of time and focus seemed to apply to the crazy minority of Marsden Grove residents as well, for they dominated all public meetings and besieged the Board of Managers with endless complaints and demands.

Nick could hardly believe that after living in Marsden Grove for about a year, Fran Walker, his immediate neighbor with whom he had become friendly, urged him to run for a spot on the community's Board of Managers. To assure continuity, one member of the five-member Board was elected each year, thereby giving each member a five-year term. "Almost as long as a United States senator," Fran joked.

As a resident Nick had quickly learned that the people who complained and bellowed the most were the least likely to offer themselves for service to the community, preferring to be the vociferous opposition. Many of the good, reasonable residents eschewed any leadership role rather than constantly be in the crosshairs of the loony malcontents.

"We need some sensible, grounded people like you," Fran had said, leaving Nick to wonder if non-sensible, lighter-than-air people comprised the current Board, with the exception of Fran as president. He was soon to find out.

He won handily against two other candidates: a lady who proposed letting wild turkeys have free range on the condo property and a man who gave a long speech on his love of the arts and how residents could bring the arts to Marsden Grove with sculptures adorning the grounds and hand-painted aquatic murals in the pool house. Half the audience was snoozing by the end of this elevated monologue.

Nick spoke briefly about his career as a corporate executive and humorously emphasized the multi-tasking abilities needed in his work. "I'd like to see our Pool House upgraded so that it could be used as a club house in all but the severe winter months," he declared, knowing this was a desire of many residents and therefore a safe, conservative platform. Scattered head-nods throughout the audience indicated ample support for this improvement.

The tally quickly indicated Nick as the winner. The candidate with aesthetic ideals was heard to mutter "Pearls before swine!" before briskly marching away.

The other three members of the five-member Board, Nick quickly learned, could have formed a vaudeville act.

John Stevens preferred to be addressed as Major, in recognition of his thirty-year career in the U.S. Marines, during which he had managed to avoid all combat duty. Used to barking orders to military subordinates, in retirement he treated everyone as his inferiors, yelling rather than speaking, and assuming in all situations that he had an unassailably correct solution to any problem.

Even sitting, the Major looked like he was standing at attention or that he suffered from some disease causing a stiffening of the spinal cord. He never spoke in any group, whether it be three or thirty, without first standing up at full attention and talking rapidly as if he were drilling soldiers or addressing battalions of troops about to take some beachhead. His patriotism had no limits and he hounded the Board to begin each meeting with the Pledge of Allegiance, to no avail. In all, he was a windup strutting, posturing tin soldier, made even more ridiculous by his five-foot-five-inch height. He was always taking offense at something or someone—a life lived in dyspeptic bluster and high dudgeon.

When the Major appeared at the community pool, his body was a startling billboard for every patriotic slogan, with tattoos saying "Semper Fi," "For God and country," "Death before dishonor," and an American flag fluttering across his scrawny chest. His filial devotion was exhibited by his "Sainted Mother" tattoo on one pusillanimous bicep and "Righteous Father" on the other. On Veterans Day he appeared in full dress uniform from morning to night, whether he was sweeping his patio, bathing his German shepherd or running an errand. His two marriages had ended in divorce and he was known to speak disdainfully of the entire female sex.

Whenever Nick encountered the Major, he always offered an intentionally sloppy salute, which the Major loved, not recognizing its mocking intent.

Jessie Knowles was another Board member deserving of star billing on any vaudeville circuit. By any standard Jessie was a giant of a man, standing many inches over six feet and weighing many pounds past the three-hundred mark. Nick often thought that on a dark night in other geographic locations Jessie could easily be mistaken for Big Foot or Sasquatch.

Perennially sloppy, Jessie wore clothes of clashing colors and musty odors that hung on him like moss on a tree. His bulk was so grand that he walked through doors sideways and at Board meetings he brought his own folding steel chair.

Fran Walker, as president and hostess of the monthly Board meetings always tried to create a convivial atmosphere by offering several snack foods for the other four members, most of which Jessie managed to devour before other members could sample them. Nick found it amusing that despite his slovenly appearance and undisguised voracious appetite, Jessie took great pains to obscure his bald dome with a careful comb-over that fooled no one. When disheveled by wind, his long strands of side hair curled wantonly around his left ear like misplaced spaghetti, dangling down to his shoulder.

Jessie's wife Martha was the exact opposite of her hulking husband: tiny in frame and stature and scrupulously neat in appearance. However, she possessed an iron will and was known to dominate her spouse. In rendering his opinions at Board meetings, Jessie frequently and unselfconsciously began his remarks with "Martha says," or "Martha feels," or "Martha thinks." Nick speculated that Jessie was enslaved to his wife who kept him supplied with stuffed pork chops, spare ribs and all succulent dishes from her Italian heritage. And probably lots of home-made fudge, pies, cakes and cookies to satisfy his acknowledged sweet tooth.

Jessie hated all domesticated animals and wanted to ban all cats, dogs, birds, rabbits, hamsters and any four-legged creatures from the community. His ardent advocacy for this interdiction put him in direct opposition, resulting in frequent clashes, with the third member of this possible vaudeville team, Jane Curtis.

Known as the Cat Lady throughout the community, Jane was obsessed with cats. A spinster of undeterminable age, Jane had five cats domiciled with her, which was three beyond the limit allowed by the community's guidelines. On any visit to her townhouse, one or two cats might be visible while the others were mewing upstairs, and Jane insisted that the noise was coming from outside. At other times she denied hearing any caterwauling completely.

In addition to maintaining her *"manage a six,"* Jane's mission in life was to feed all the feral cats roaming the neighborhood. This, too, was forbidden by the condo's by-laws, but Jane circumvented this rule by trudging to the end of the condo's property line late at night and leaving food for the feral felines living in the hundred-acre Preserve abutting the east end of the community. Of course, this expanse of land was home to many other creatures of the night, all of whom were attracted to Jane's free meal. The competition was fierce, and howls, screams and dying shrieks rang out in the night's silence, causing alarm and sleepless hours for many residents whose townhouses adjoined the Preserve.

Jane's obsession was evident everywhere in her condo, including her doormat with a smiling kitty and the instruction, "Please wipe your paws." Inside, cat statues, cat pictures, cat oil paintings and numerous ceramic plaques attesting to the superiority of cats suffocated the home. Jane was mostly placid and mild-mannered, if a bit too garrulous, at Board meetings except when Jessie raised any topic dealing with animals. Then, like some female version of Superman, she roared into action, transformed into a powerhouse of defensive rage and copious spittle. Jessie usually cowered before this transmogrification, much to Nick's secret amusement. She was like the mouse that roared, scaring the giant silly.

Nick could picture the vaudeville bill featuring The Major, The Goofy Giant (whom Nick secretly referred to as Big Foot), and The Cat Lady. Fran Walker had nominated Nick for Board Vice President immediately after his election. The Major had objected, but since nobody liked him, his ambition to be a Board leader was again thwarted, deepening his agitated bluster. Cat Lady served as Board secretary

Nick had quickly come to realize exactly what Fran Walker meant when she had spoken about having sensible, grounded people join the Board. Unfortunately, he and Fran were in the minority.

More people were now trooping in as the temperature under the canvas top soared, along with Nick's uncertainty about what the next few hours might bring. Like any military man, he felt that he had to mentally prepare himself for the predictable skirmishes to come, as Marsden Grove's foot soldiers marched in, seemingly ready and eager for battle.

2

The seats were now filling up rapidly and the other Board members were all in place behind a long table facing the audience. Nick saw that the Cat Lady was wearing a blouse imprinted with faces of kittens and that Big Foot still had crumbs on his straggly mustache from breakfast. Fran Walker looked crisp and cool in shorts and a T-shirt that flattered her trim figure, while the Major wore an olive T-shirt, fatigue pants and heavy boots as if he were going on maneuvers. Nick was dressed in khaki pants and a golf shirt.

We probably should have brought mace or pepper spray, Nick thought, half in earnest when recalling the fist fight that had broken out at last year's annual meeting between two men who had adjacent townhouses and were constantly feuding over noise issues and one man's dog pooping on the other man's patio.

Nick knew that no meeting would be complete without a barrage of petty complaints from those residents who perpetually saw the glass as half empty and expected perfection in every aspect of life at Marsden Grove. Nick marveled at how seniors could muster such heightened indignation and heat over trivial details like the lids of their garbage cans not being put back properly after garbage had been collected, or the soda in the soda machine by the pool house not being cold enough. The irate speeches they made to the Board invariably contained the words "unacceptable" and "I demand," with all public utterances delivered in a confrontational tone.

Nick couldn't fathom how these dyspeptic people seemed to live their lives in a perpetually dissatisfied and agitated state, searching for minor issues to vent their disgruntlement, oblivious to the blessings they enjoyed of longevity and prosperity. To spend their retirement years in beautiful, secure homes in beautiful surroundings, with many stimulating and gregarious neighbors, never seemed to moderate their negativity.

Nick saw Fran glance at her watch and rise to bring the meeting to order. He took a deep breath, steeling himself for almost anything that might happen. The first order of business was voting on the proposed budget for the coming fiscal year. This always started the fireworks popping.

"Good morning. Let's get the meeting started before it gets any hotter and we have to relocate it to the pool," Fran said in her pretend cheerful voice, as though she were going to lead the group in a camp roundelay and this was going to be a lark. "I hope you've all picked up a copy of our budget proposal."

Half a dozen hands shot up like exploding rockets and began flapping in the air, competing strenuously for recognition. Before Fran could recognize anyone, Dagmar Neilson was out of her chair, shouting in a thick Swedish accent that she never seemed to lose despite her having been brought to the States as a young girl. Nick watched with fascination as the veins in Dagmar's neck popped out like docking ropes and her face, always blotchy, now turned crimson.

"It's absolutely disgraceful that we are still not recycling," she shouted, indignation punctuating every word. Nick privately agreed with her, although she always spoke in such a heated, condescending manner that her words were lost on most of her audience, alienated by her offensive delivery. Her angry grimaces always reminded him of a portrait of Medusa he had seen somewhere, everything but the twisting snakes for hair. By her third sentence she was all fired up, in full throttle.

Fran, with her small, high-pitched voice, was no match, so she waved both arms and shouted, "We know, Dagmar, and we are hoping to find another carting company that will pick up recyclables without doubling our cost."

"The cost be damned!" Dagmar indignantly retorted, hurling a withering look directly at Fran. "This should be your number-one priority!"

"Not at the expense of keeping our grounds looking nice and helping our resale values," Vera Parks shouted from her seat in the rear of the audience. Nick knew that Mrs. Parks had long had her unit on the market since her husband died. She was asking an inflated price, wouldn't compromise and was getting low-bid offers which she ascribed to everything but her own unrealistic appraisal of the current market.

"In the meantime, keep your hands out of my garbage!" Jack Skelly bellowed angrily, standing with hands defiantly on hips.

Dagmar turned in Jack's direction and hurled him another one of her withering stares. She was often seen going among the townhomes, retrieving cans and bottles from other residents' garbage bins and depositing them in a large sack slung over her shoulder like a bedraggled Santa Claus. In acid tones Dagmar responded with a distinct curl of her lip, "All your discarded pornographic magazines should be recycled."

Explosive audience gasp! Nick chuckled to himself as he thought of all the rumors and gossip that rampantly spread across the Marsden Grove community, comprised of so many seniors with so much time on their hands and so little to do. This newest revelation would keep the phone lines buzzing for days.

"Stay the hell away from my can!" a crimson-faced and clearly embarrassed Jack yelled before quickly sitting down.

Dagmar would have continued excoriating the community for its ecological deficiencies, but another booming voice out-shouted hers. "Why are we spending more money to power-wash the buildings again. We did that about six years ago. Let's cover the cedar siding with vinyl and be done with it."

Dagmar, who had never sat down, responded in her typically arch tone, "The perfect way to ruin the aesthetic appeal of this community!"

Vera Parks jumped to her feet. "And ruin our resale value!"

In a split-second lull amidst the shouting, a low, cultured voice grabbed the air: "May I say something?" Celeste Grayson asked politely. Fran Walker, happy to have a moment of quiet, nodded. Celeste stood, as other women took in her simple, finely tailored and expensive-looking dress, set off by a silk neck scarf intertwining with her two-strand pearl necklace. Her ensemble presented a stark contrast to the slacks, shorts, muumuus and bathing suits of the other females in the audience.

Everyone knew that after her husband died, Celeste had sold her big house in the Hamptons and moved into the largest townhouse at the end of the complex, facing the woods. Stories abounded about the incredible improvements she had made, based on all the trucks and workmen at her door for months, to the point where the gossip had her place resembling the interior of Versailles. No-one could speak with any authority, however, because Celeste only had guests from outside the community and delivered a frosty "Good Day" to any neighbors she briefly encountered, discouraging any familiarity.

A young woman had moved in with her shortly after her arrival, and everyone assumed that she was a relative. This, too, was conjecture since the young woman was seldom seen and Celeste was far too imperious in manner for anyone to pose a direct personal question.

As all eyes turned in her direction, Celeste spoke in a style that Nick thought was mock-British royalty: slowly, enunciating each syllable, with strangely accented words that made her speech sound, first, southern, then Welch, and, at other points, Hungarian—everything but Icelandic. For all its odd affectations, Nick could see from the audience's rapt attention that this was a totally mesmerizing performance.

"I believe," she said and paused, as if she were about to address a joint Congressional session, "that we should consider investing in a removable dome to cover our three tennis courts. This would give us the advantage of being able to play tennis year-round and this could also enhance our property values." Stroking her pearls absent-mindedly, she added, "I know many upscale communities in the Hamptons' area that have done this," and sat down.

A stunned silence followed her delivery. Nick was again chuckling to himself. If the Virgin Mary had suddenly appeared in their midst and asked them to pray for world peace and promised an end to tooth decay and baldness, the effect could not have been more stunning.

Celeste had never been seen near the tennis courts, which were usually vacant most of the spring, summer and fall days except for a small clique of residents who also exhibited snooty tribal tendencies. In the midst of all the fractious controversy over snow removal, garbage collection, tree pruning, walkway repaving, pool house refurbishment, assigned parking and shingle power-washing, to suddenly drop this topic on the crowd left them dumbfounded.

Fran Walker quickly seized the moment with a chirpy, "Thank you," and was about to ask for a vote on the budget when she saw the hand of retired police officer Bill Russell go up, and she nodded in his direction.

"Madame President," Bill intoned formally, "what about our recent suicide?"

A deadly silence descended on the crowd. Nick felt his shoulder muscles tensing as he sensed they were entering into unchartered territory that could spell havoc. All eyes, some agitated, some confused, some alarmed, turned toward the five Board members, all of whom were taken completely by surprise.

3

"I'll repeat my question, Madame President," Bill Russell said in an even louder voice, ringing with self-importance. "What about the recent suicide here at Marsden Grove?"

Bill was referring to the most shocking event ever to occur in the community when a resident went to check on an elderly neighbor, Emma Craig, and found her hanging from a crossbeam spanning the cathedral ceiling in her living room. She had evidently stood on a chair and then kicked it away. Of course, it made the headlines of the local paper.

Occurring only three days earlier, Emma's suicide had been a hot topic in the community as people gossiped and speculated why she had taken her life. Everything from an incurable disease to bankruptcy and a broken heart—her husband had passed away two years earlier—was offered by idle tongues with scant facts and vivid imaginations, secretly thrilled to be peripherally involved in such a shocking event.

Emma's only daughter had come to claim the body, and the hubbub was only beginning to decline until Bill Russell raised the topic.

Fran Walker's small, bird-like features seemed to cave in as she looked around the room with a conflictive stare. Nick decided to come to her rescue, entering the void with "What about the suicide?"

"Well," Bill intoned solemnly, enjoying the cynosure of all eyes, "I've spoken to the detective who investigated the scene and there seems to be some troubling details surrounding the case."

A startled buzz skittered across the crowd.

"I'm not aware of this," was all Fran, clearly flustered, could muster weakly.

A louder buzz, as people shifted in their seats and exchanged comments among their neighbors. Hoping to quell any mounting anxiety, Nick spoke again. "The Board is not aware of this, and I don't believe anything has been mentioned of an untoward nature to her only daughter."

Bill Russell shot back, "That's not what I heard! We should all be informed."

"Are you suggesting foul play?" Fran asked with noticeable incredulity in her tone.

"All I'm saying at this point," Bill said, his voice swelling for dramatic impact, "is that the ongoing investigation is raising some questions that might—I say **migh**t—lead to a different conclusion than suicide."

A cacophony of startled voices thundered across the throng. Fran seemed frozen with indecision as to how to respond to this explosive declaration, so Nick again stepped in. "Thank you, Bill. When the investigation is completed, we'll inform the community of its findings, but while it's ongoing, there's clearly no information to share with the public. Let's move on with our agenda."

Nick saw from the roiling agitation sweeping across the residents that the genii of suspicion and fear was already out of the bottle. The clamor of the erupting crowd and the frightened looks on many of the ladies' faces, as well as on a few of the men's, showed the full alarm Bob's incendiary words had provoked.

The Major now jumped to his feet, fanning the flames. "We've got to get to the bottom of this immediately!" he shouted, as though he had just learned that Russia was hatching a secret plan to invade Marsden Grove. "I'll personally investigate this matter and report to the community."

Nick retorted quietly but firmly. "That's generous of you, Major, but before anyone goes off half-cocked, let's first learn the details from the authorities and not assume anything until the Board has those details."

The Major harrumphed but said no more. He knew that Nick had done two tours of duty in Vietnam as a helicopter pilot and been shot down twice, while he, the Major, was occupying a cushy desk job back in the States throughout that entire bloody war. And the Major knew that Nick knew about his inglorious career; consequently, Nick was the one man who could effectively shut the Major up.

The topic was, for the moment, dropped but obviously not dismissed in the minds of most. Nick wrote himself a note to get the detective's name from Bill Russell and call that person on Monday.

Now other residents rose to address their pet issues: the sidewalks needing repaving; the parking spaces needed their lines repainted; the pool house needed a thorough cleaning; more exercise equipment was needed in the gym section of the pool house; more games like ping pong were needed in the pool house for when the grandchildren visited; more comfortable furniture was needed in the pool house; another shower was needed in the pool house.

Nick thought that if all these things were added to the pool house, there'd be no room for people, but, like Fran, he listened and nodded his head.   He tried to look attentively at each speaker, no matter how garrulous or boring, by focusing on their moving lips until he was caught up in a fantasy of dancing, puckering, crunching lips racing along at hyper speed which he set to the tune of *Alexander's Ragtime Band*.   Then he caught himself almost chuckling and returned fully to reality.

A vote was finally taken and the budget was passed, but not before David Longstreet had delivered his annual harangue on the need for additional economizing to avoid an increase in the monthly maintenance fee next year.   Fran Walker patiently pointed out that the increase for the coming year was only two percent, as it had been for the present year.   David countered by stating that we didn't need such a big reserve fund for emergencies, and Nick responded that they had only the minimum reserve fund mandated by New York State law.

Unbowed, David suggested that we didn't need all the snow ploughing since hardly any resident went to work and we could wait a day or two for the snow to melt.

Nick stood up. "And if a resident needed emergency help or we had a fire on the premises after a heavy snow, how would we feel if the ambulance or fire truck was blocked from entering our property? They can't come in by dog sled!"

Low ripples of laughter from the audience. Longstreet did not give up. "Why do we need all the help we have?" he asked defiantly.

Fran now took the lead. "Gillie Zamiksovitch is our only full-time worker and we have two part-time workers on an as-needed basis. That seems like very few when you consider our number of units is over one-hundred-forty. And consider, too, the extent of our property and the constant need for both maintenance and repairs."

The Major shot to his feet as though an explosion had gone off in his chair. Speaking in his usual rapid-fire volley of words, he said, "I will personally join with Mr. Longstreet in reviewing all expenditures and seeing where we might save more money and report back to the community."

Nick was fed up with all the Major's posturing. With a deadly serious expression and a low voice harboring a menacing tone, he rose again and directly faced the Major who was standing on the other side of the seated Fran. "As a member of this Board, Major, you participated fully in all our budgetary meetings."

"But I objected to some things," the Major shouted, not daring to look directly at Nick but currying favor from the audience with his smart-alecky smile.

"Yes, you did. As I remember, you wanted to discontinue using our lawn sprinklers and rely on Mother Nature. And you didn't want to repair the toilet in the pool house because you said people could run back to their homes and use their own bathrooms—wet bathing suits be damned!"

Clearly disapproving mumbles from the audience. The Major was wilting. Nick continued.

"In the end, we did what all Boards do. We voted on each and every item and the majority approved the budget. We think it's fair and reasonable. We'll continue to monitor all expenses with a sharp eye for any place we can save money. After all, it's our money, too."

Smattering of applause. Nick and the Major both sat down, but the Major couldn't resist one parting, pathetic shot. "I'll be extra vigilant."

Yeah, Nick thought. *If you had your way, you'd fire all the help and mobilize the residents to tend the grounds under your command. You'd close the pool and tennis courts and organize forced marches for exercise. You pathetic, megalomaniacal phony!*

Nick's internal monologue was interrupted as Fran moved on to the next agenda item. For two hours, with continuous wrangling, rancor, bloviating and free disassociation, the meeting continued in physical and emotional heat. Whenever any speaker did not speak directly into the hand-held portable microphone, several residents with hearing impairments would shout, "Speak up! We can't hear you!" or "Speak directly into the mike!"

Several times the Reverend Tom Snyder spoke, or, more accurately, preached, about the need for coming together. His mini-sermons fell on deaf ears because all his public pronouncements were rendered in a righteous, all-knowing and pompous monotone that undercut anything he said. The Reverend never opened his mouth without making Nick feel instantly sleepy. Nick could never imagine Reverend Tom bringing anyone closer to God, except maybe Tom, himself, but then, Nick thought, even God would probably get bored.

In terms of self-inflated egos, Nick placed Tom just below the Major and just ahead of Dr. Carlton Wright, a retired psychologist who was endlessly offering esoteric interpretations of people's actions and the roots of their hostility. Fortunately, Dr. Wright was not present at this meeting or, Nick reflected, it would have been extended by another hour.

To Nick, all three of these men truly loved the sound of their own voices and seemed to perform in an echo chamber that mirrored their own reflection and inflated self-importance. Nick secretly called this posturing triumvirate the Three Stooges: Officious, Pious and Gaseous.

The meeting finally ended, more from exhaustion than accomplishment. The temperature was now hovering around ninety and many people eagerly adjourned to the pool.

During the exodus Nick spied Shirley Grant, the reporter for the local newspaper. She was going against the human tide and heading straight for the Board members. Confronting Fran, she asked, "Have you anything to say about the possibility of foul play in connection with the supposed suicide of ...." Shirley paused and looked down at her notes. "...of Emma Craig?"

Like a deer caught in the headlights, Fran was both speechless and immobile, her eyes staring fixedly at Shirley as if she had just been asked how many abortions had she performed in her spare time. Standing next to Fran, Nick hastened to relieve the silence with "We have nothing to say at this time. A suicide is considered a crime and the investigation is ongoing."

"But Officer Russell..." Shirley began, but Nick cut her off. "Officer Russell is speaking for himself and not for the community. I repeat, we have no comment."

Taking Fran by the arm, Nick led her away. "Thank you, Nick," she said quietly as they emerged from under the canvas top. "Bill Russell's statement really threw me. Do you think it's true—that the police suspect foul play?" Fran's voice was quivering with this last question.

Nick sought to soothe Fran. "Maybe there are some minor details that the police have to clear up before they finalize a report. I wouldn't jump to conclusions, as Bill seems to be doing. Let's wait and see."

"I suppose you're right," Fran said with little conviction. "Thanks for all your help." She headed toward the pool.

Nick could feel the perspiration dripping down his sides. As refreshing as a dip in the pool might seem, he knew he'd be bombarded with questions and further complaints and he'd had enough for one day. Hell, how about one year? How about one lifetime? He hastened toward his townhouse where Christina would be waiting. The problems of the last hellacious hours receded as lust took center stage.

4

Three years after Judy's death and his subsequent move to Marsden Grove, Nick felt the itch but wasn't sure how to scratch it. He acknowledged that while Judy's memory was a constant in his daily thoughts, he now wanted a woman in his life. He missed the intimacy more than sex but wanted sex, too, and if this made him a dirty old man at sixty-six, so be it!

His golf buddy, George Perkins, had been divorced twice and for several years had raved about the women he met on internet dating services. George, at sixty-four, liked to play the field and had no intention of marrying for a third time, so he gladly settled for short-term, intimate and thrilling relationships that always dissolved when any woman hinted of a permanent commitment.

What amazed Nick was George's recounting of so many women, or "babes" as George called them, who, like him, were only interested in short-term shack-ups and no strings. George also spoke proudly of younger women, some even in their thirties, who liked older men as long as they still looked decent, had money to spend and were good in the sack.

George was a good-looking man, outgoing and financially secure, who kept himself reasonably fit with lots of golf and what he described as "bedroom gymnastics." He had spent a fortune on having hair plugs surgically shifted from the side of his head to the bald spot on his crown, and he dressed fastidiously. As to his bedroom performance, to hear George tell it, he was a cross between Sly Stallone and Errol Flynn. Even discounting braggadocio, Nick could see why the ladies went for George.

Nick had decided it was time for a stark inventory. Naked, he stood in front of a full-length mirror and confronted himself. His five-foot-ten-inch frame was carrying only about ten to twelve pounds over his ideal weight, and this extra poundage was barely noticeable when he sucked his stomach in. He practiced doing this several times, resembling an accordion playing The Flight of the Bumble Bee. Then he realized that he could not permanently suck it in without eventually turning blue or passing out, so he resolved to return to a daily exercise regimen and cut back on take-out pizzas, barbecue chicken wings and desserts.

His light brown hair was still thick, with no hairline creep, although it was streaked with gray at the temples. Well, didn't that give him a distinguished air, like the men in the TV ads for Viagra? Which, thankfully, he knew he didn't need, based on the recurring sensual dreams he was having and the happy but frustrating state of arousal he discovered upon waking.

His teeth were beyond good; they were great—gleamingly white and perfectly even. Judy had always told him she loved his dazzling smile. Now he studied his reflection as he practiced smiling several times, from slight smiles, lips slightly parted, to half smiles, lips agape, to full, open-mouth, all-teeth-bared smiles. He was pleased with each display. He'd have to remember to smile a lot on first meeting any date, without appearing like a happy simpleton.

Judy had also praised his warm, hazel eyes, and he resolved to stare directly into the eyes of his date but not too intently, he cautioned himself, lest he look like an ax murderer choosing his next victim.

It had been so long since he had dated and given any thought to his appearance or the impression he might be making on any new lady that he clearly had to muster his resources and relearn the art of flirting in the new century.

All in all, he armored himself with a renewed sense of tentative confidence as he started a new adventure of late mid-life dating. Or was it old-age dating? He couldn't be sure, but he was eager to begin his exploration of meeting ladies in the modern technological age.

5

Nick selected an internet match-up service recommended by George for its "hot babes," paid the entrance fee and filled out the biographical form. He had read George's profile and quickly decided to take a more conservative, less vaunting tone.

While George had described himself as "wealthy, very handsome, superbly fit and very sensual," Nick used "nice looking, decent shape, solvent and warm nature" for his profile. Where George had said "seeking amorous adventures and intense thrills," Nick preferred "looking for companionship and possibly long-term commitment."

In the section asking the type of woman he was seeking, Nick again eschewed George's description of "buff body and athletic." Since Nick knew that golf was the principal exercise George ever engaged in, and his was the lazy man's way, riding on his golf cart, always accompanied by a caddy, what was all the emphasis on "athletic" about? Was that a code word for limberness in the bedroom? Nick decided not to ask George. George's ideal female companion, according to what he had written, in addition to athletic prowess, would be "lushly attractive, action-oriented, confident, fun-loving, intelligent, unencumbered, financially secure, uninhibited and ready for all new experiences."

It seemed clear to Nick that George wanted a woman rivaling a Miss Universe, with all the requisite attributes and attitudes that so often accompanied the made-up profile of a beauty queen—everything except "deeply religious and desiring world peace," but that wouldn't fit with "uninhibited." Upon further reflection Nick decided that George's description could easily fit a very high-priced hooker or "call girl."

Giving careful thought to describing the type of woman he was looking for, Nick wrote "attractive, middle-age woman" (eliminating, he hoped, the young ladies with father fixations or looking for a sugar daddy), "warm, upbeat, good sense of humor, compassionate." He then decided to add "political and social liberal," since he knew he wouldn't be compatible with fervent evangelicals or Tea Party enthusiasts, ardent libertarian members of the National Rifle Association, opponents of gay rights or deniers of climate change. Thanks to Judy's influence over their many years together, Nick had changed from being a conservative—even snobby—Republican to seeing the world through Judy's compassionate eyes and embracing diversity and heterodoxy.

The picture of George accompanying his profile must have been taken ten years earlier and then done by a professional photographer and extensively touched up, hiding the hint of jowls, the slightly receding hairline and a delicately incipient paunch. It resembled the present George about as much as Eleanor Roosevelt, on her best day, resembled Marilyn Monroe.

"Don't just show a headshot," George had warned Nick. "They want to see the whole package."

Nick thought that George took his own advice to extremes with a picture of himself in a tank top and skimpy shorts, posed with chest and shoulders swelled, arms flexed and fists tightened, in that classic stance of a professional weight lifter. The photographer must have cropped at least ten inches off of George's waist, giving him the incongruous look of a cross between Arnold Schwarzenegger and Sophia

Loren. And speaking of package, Nick couldn't help noticing that George was blatantly advertising his wares, which, thanks either to trick photography or enhanced stuffing, could have been a contender for the Guinness Book of Records.

Nick chose a recent picture of himself that a friend had shot, showing him in a casual pose on a golf course, squinting into the sun with a full smile displaying those great pearly whites.

Within twenty-four hours after his completed profile and picture were posted, the responses started coming. A week later he decided that either the women couldn't read or he should have simply written "Open to all females, eighteen to eighty, regardless of physical condition, emotional stability, mental impediments, police records or other romantic entanglements."

From the cavalcade of responses he received, he concluded that the world was a very sad place, populated by legions of desperately lonely or screwed-up women seeking solace, validation or financial support from strangers. But then he quickly learned that there was another type of woman who, like George, was looking exclusively for thrills and temporary bed partners.

George had warned him, "You have to wade through the frogs before you find a princess." From the instant responses he was receiving, Nick saw the truth in this remark. He would have to make his way carefully through this briery thicket.

The first response he received to his profile was from Robin.

"Hi. I like your picture. The photo with my profile was taken about ten years ago, just before my fiancé broke off our engagement and I started a Hagen Daas marathon and eventually gained a hundred pounds. I use this picture to motivate me to get back to my ideal weight. I've lost over fifteen pounds and want the men to see what I look like at my best if they would be willing to help me lose the rest of the weight. Not a bad looker, right?"

Nick studied Robin's ten-year-old picture showing a woman appearing to be mid-forties, not bad looking and with a full but appealing figure. Then he mentally added eighty-five pounds to the woman and cringed. He remembered a picture he had seen of a grossly overweight Elizabeth Taylor whom, as a younger woman, he had considered the most beautiful girl in the world. This particular picture showed

Liz with many extra pounds looking like that magnificent mound of flesh from *Star Wars*, Jabba the Hutt. She was practically unrecognizable except for the eyebrows. Nick shuddered and deleted Robin's message.

Quickly Nick scanned the six other messages lined up after Robin's, first looking at the picture of each lady. He deleted two for looking much older than they claimed to be. Either they were lying or life had treated them very harshly. Another picture showed a lady with several missing front teeth who was unselfconsciously smiling broadly. She actually listed her work as "hog butcher and professional laundress." Her profile said she loved hunting, bowling and country music and riding behind a man on a Harley Davidson. Judging from her picture, Nick guessed that some of the rides on the "hog" had ended disastrously. DELETED.

Another lady, whose internet moniker was Evensong, passed the physical test in terms of looking attractive, pleasant and the right age category. Nick liked her profile and responded to her. After several more exchanges, the lady confessed that her two husbands had both committed suicide. A warning bell went off in Nick's head. DELETED.

The next picture took his breath away. The woman, dubbed Belle, was a knock-out and looked to be in her thirties. Her message said "Hi, if you're looking for a hot babe who likes older men and loves to party and have fun, both outdoors and indoors, hit me back." Little was included on her profile except her height—a statuesque five-feet-ten-inches "in heels," and her measurements, "36—24—38." Under the type of man she preferred, she had stated, "older, fun-loving and generous." His libido kicking in, Nick was tempted to pursue this lady but then decided that Belle was more suited for George than for him. DELETED.

Several weeks went by as Nick received more emails from ladies who, for one reason or another, he deemed unsuitable. He had initiated his own search, choosing a few categories to limit his sampling of profiles. One lady seemed perfect for looks, stated age, interests and a great sense of humor displayed in her return emails. Unfortunately, she lived in South Africa. "It would be fun to have a boyfriend in the States," she had written, "and you could visit me here." For Nick, who didn't like flying, that wasn't the same as living in Pennsylvania or Ohio, and that kind of long-distance relationship held no appeal. DELETED.

A slew of Asian ladies from exotic-sounding places offered marriage as their goal. Their pictures revealed either leering, tired faces suggesting a lot of unsavory history in their backgrounds, or fresh, juvenile visages that looked too young for anything but formal adoption. ALL DELETED.

Nick was giving up hope of ever finding some suitable woman when magic finally struck.

6

Late one night when Nick had spent too much time reading and deleting unsuitable profiles, a lady by the name of Christina appeared on his screen. Her headshot showed a woman with neat blond hair, blue-gray eyes and a wide, smiling mouth. Her profile was equally arresting: Age 56, widowed, elementary school teacher, one child 26 (living in Europe).

The words she used to describe the kind of man and the relationship she was looking for were many of the same words that he had used in describing his desired woman, including "good sense of humor." What reinforced his intuitive feeling that he had hit the jackpot was her listing golf as her major sports activity.

Several emails back and forth, much shared humor and small confessions, and then they were on the phone, chatting comfortably like old friends. The additional pictures she sent him with her emails revealed a nice, if generous, figure, relieving him of his desire to lose his extra pounds.   Serendipitously, she lived in a Long Island community only about a half-hour away.

Since they both had expressed a fondness for Mexican food, their first date was at a Mexican restaurant half-way between their homes. Christina was everything in person that he had come to expect from all he had learned about her to date.   And something more.   The hard facts were now supplemented by the warm attention she gave him when he spoke, by the gentle touch of her long, slender fingers on his arm to emphasize some point she was making, by the sheen of her skin and the throaty laughter that magnified her glowing personality.   When she retreated to the Ladies Room, he took note of her shapely legs.

To his delight, he learned that her deceased husband had been a golf nut and had introduced her to the game, which she had taken up avidly, and they had played at least twice a week during the golfing season. Their mutual mishaps on the golf course became a topic of bemused conversation, evoking much laughter. At one point she interrupted their laughter and exclaimed, "You have such beautiful teeth!" and he could feel his chest swelling with pleasure.

If Cinderella's fairy godmother, who did such wonders for Cinderella's state of mind as well as her future, had taken a personal interest in Nick, he now felt that she could not have done a better job than in sending him Christina. Their unexpected, relaxed intimacy, which he had only experienced with his beloved Judy, was startling in its easy, natural flow, leaving him positively giddy with delight.

They talked about their deceased spouses—Christina's husband, Jeff. had died at sixty-two of prostate cancer—with unselfconscious candor and warmth, for it was clear that they had both been in very loving relationships. Christina's only child, Garth, was an architect working in Italy for an international company.

They met at seven and were still talking, still thoroughly engrossed in each other, still discovering attractive personal nuances when the restaurant closed at eleven. Dizzy from realizing he could feel such unexpected euphoria with this lady, he acknowledged to himself that he was smitten. He walked her to her car. She unlocked the door and turned toward him, smiling, and then, in a spontaneously natural gesture, she kissed him on the lips quickly and said, "Thank you for this wonderful evening."

Nick hadn't expected this quick motion and he wanted to wrap his arms around her and go on kissing her, but she eluded his embrace and slid into her car. Smiling brightly up at him she said "Call me," and started the engine. He stood there like some befuddled teenager, tongue-tied and tranquilized, shacking his head like a bubblehead doll and smiling inanely as she drove off.

As he walked to his car, Nick almost skipped with joy. He kept thinking that this was too good to be true, that this was like scenes of first meetings in cheap romance novels, which he could only imagine since he hadn't read any, where everything had gone so smoothly and enticingly. He couldn't wait to see Christina again.

For their fourth date she invited him back to her home, a cottage in a beachfront community on the north shore of Long Island. Half the residents, she explained, were full-time and the other half only came in the summer and early fall. "It's always quiet in the winter," she noted. Indeed, as they had driven up, Nick noticed that while the houses were check by jowl, there were no lights in the neighboring houses on this cold March night.

Christina's cottage, she explained, had been a ramshackle leftover from the '30s when she and her husband had bought and revitalized it. Now, with an open great room encompassing a living room, dining area and galley kitchen, plus two bedrooms and a large deck with a stunning view of the Long Island Sound, it was, Nick immediately felt, attractive and cozy.

"I hope you like Italian food," she said from the kitchen after settling him on a sofa with a glass of wine and lighting the stacked kindling in the stone fireplace. "My husband ▓▓▓▓ was Italian and loved his Italian food so that's what I became proficient at."

Nick couldn't believe his ears. He responded brightly, "My father's mother was Italian and my dad loved Italian food. My mother, who was Irish and Welch, made a lot of Italian dishes when I was growing up, which I loved. My father used to joke that if they didn't have ravioli and manicotti and spaghetti in heaven, he'd prefer not to go there."

In short order they were seated in the dining nook enjoying lasagna, tossed salad, warm garlic bread and more wine. A record of Chopin's etudes was playing softly in the background, and the table candles lent interesting shadows to Christina's face.

"I try to avoid desserts," Christina confessed, "but I have ice cream and chocolate sauce if that appeals to you."

"I can afford to skip desserts, too," a smiling Nick replied, patting his stomach, now full after two servings of lasagna.

"Then let's have coffee and brandy by the fireplace," she suggested, rising from the table and collecting the dinnerware.

Without asking, Nick imitated her actions and, together, they quickly cleared the table, which reminded him of the routine that he and Judy always followed: she did the cooking and he did the cleaning up. He found it very pleasurable to be working in tandem again. He quickly stacked the dishes in the dishwasher while she arranged a tray with a coffee carafe, two mugs, cream and sugar, a bottle of Hennessy cognac and two snifters.

They retreated to the sofa, not talking, just enjoying the fire after Christina had added some logs and slowly sipping their brandy.

Despite his relaxed appearance, Nick's mind was frenzied. This evening's entire scene, the cozy cottage, the food and wine and then brandy by the roaring fire, all made him feel like Cary Grant in some Hollywood romantic movie. But unlike Cary Grant, who was always suave and in command of all situations, Nick was as nervous as a teenager on a first date whose thoughts fermented with desire but was unsure of how to execute the right moves.

It had been so long since he had been with a woman other than his "comfortable-as-an-old-shoe" wife that he wasn't sure how to behave. His confusion and hesitancy must have been perceptible to Christina who, sipping the last drop in her brandy snifter and staring into the fireplace, said softly, "Nick, you're welcome to spend the night."

The gong struck, the bells went off, the fireworks exploded, Chopin was replaced with *Stars and Stripes Forever and he was told he could pass Go and collect his two hundred dollars. His mind shut down, surrendering to his libido.* Lunging across the short distance separating them on the sofa, he embraced her.

Christina gave a loud yelp and sprung from the sofa. Rampant confusion overtook him. What was wrong? What cues had he misread? Looking up with the expression of a befuddled little boy, he saw her standing there, laughing.

"I'm sorry," she blurted between continued spurts of laughter. Then she turned away from him and he saw it: a long stain down the back of her dress from neck to waist. She pointed to his right arm, dangling over the back of the sofa. His hand was still clutching his brandy snifter. In his impetuous, mad dash to embrace her, he had forgotten about his brandy glass and had tipped its remaining contents down the back of her dress.

"At least the brandy was warm," she said, her laughter replaced with a warm smile. Now he could smile, too, while uttering, "I'm so sorry," but flooded with relief that he had not committed some egregiously offensive act that repulsed her and destabilized this idyllic evening.

"I better get out of this dress," she said, smiling provocatively at him. Encouraged, he said, "Let me help you," and they were off.

The quick hop to the bedroom, the shucking of clothes, the tangling of bodies and the ensuing romps across the king-size bed were wondrous acts leaving him spent and mystified. He could not believe what had just happened.

In his sixty-six years of living, he was not without carnal experience, ranging from teenage fumbling and probing to his military years with easy pick-ups and, yes, paid couplings. He had been completely satisfied with his sex life with Judy and had only occasionally felt any overt temptation, but he had never strayed. Yet, now, with Christina, he had discovered an entirely new type of woman: a lovely, refined, genteel professional woman who was a cyclone of libidinous urgings and inventive moves in the sack.

He almost chuckled to himself as he thought of some old bromidic saying about what every man wanted in a woman: a whiz in the kitchen, an angel in the nursery and a harlot in the bedroom. Creative sex positions he had mentally imagined as a surging youth, he had now actually experienced.

Magically, she had encouraged him to release all his inhibitions and he was more aggressive, more audacious and more gymnastic than he thought himself capable of, at his age. It felt like they were romping through page after page of the *Karma Sutra*, with many more delightful pages to look forward to. Although he hadn't smoked in forty years, he suddenly craved a cigarette as a symbolic act ending this night of glorious debauchery. She had turned this staid, conventional man into a rollicking, romping Don Juan.

He was extremely pleased with himself, as though he had looked in the mirror and discovered a younger, handsomer face smiling back; he was also very grateful to this amazing woman for liberating him from any residual puritanical shackles. His total fulfillment led to a paradoxical state of blissful emptiness, and, drained of all energy, he lay listlessly on the bed, smiling vacuously like someone lobotomized.

From that night on, they were a bonded couple. He spent at least two week-nights at her cottage and she joined him in his townhouse on weekends. On her first visit to his home he waited expectantly to see if she would pass the one remaining litmus test, a very important one: Charley.

From the time he was five years old and had gotten a puppy for his birthday, dogs had been constant, loving and loyal companions in Nick's life. While each dog in the ensuing years was fondly remembered for a distinct personality and vexatious traits, his current dog, Charley, seemed to possess a preternatural intelligence that allowed him to read Nick's mind and interpret his moods. Judy had surprised Nick with Charley as a mewling four-week-old bundle of chocolate fur, and now, six years later, the dog and master were inseparable.

Always eager to meet visitors, Charley had romped to the front door as Nick and Christina entered, rendering his usual signs of delight upon Nick's return and then curiously sniffing Christina. Christina had immediately sunk to her knees and said "Hello Charley," as she scratched his silky ruff.

Charley liked her voice and especially liked her vigorous scratching. He looked into her eyes and she stared warmly into his. Like his master, Charley was quickly smitten. His tail wagged tumultuously and he bestowed a quick, wet kiss on Christina's cheek, a distinct sign of total acceptance, not bestowed lightly or indiscrim-inately. Nick was delighted with the instant rapport that Christina seemed to establish with Charley.

In the ensuing months, Nick and Christina's sexual romps continued unabated and uninhibited as they found new interior locations for their spontaneous combustion: every place but the pantry—too small and all those dangerous canned goods, they concluded—and the deck—too public, although that added the fillip of a dangerous tryst, they admitted, intrigued.

Meanwhile, beyond their sensual hijinks, their compatibility ratio on other fronts increased. After only several months since meeting Christina, Nick was already giving thought to marriage. A few hints that she had dropped suggested she didn't feel ready for that binding commitment, and he didn't push it. How could he, with everything he currently had?

As he headed toward his townhouse, hot and tired after the exhausting Annual Homeowners Meeting, he wanted a cool drink and a shower. Then he thought of Christina washing his back and pressing her pillowy breasts against him. His fantasies took off and his pace quickened. The Lone Ranger Rides Again! Hi, Ho, Silver!

7

All of Nick's fantasies were squelched when he arrived home and found Bill Russell, the retired city cop, waiting for him on the front porch.

"It's important that we talk privately," Bill said gruffly.

Bill could only be described as a burly man, whose barrel chest still extended beyond his bulging gut. A shaved head, ruddy complexion and eighteen-inch neck atop a six-foot frame completed the intimidating picture.

When any accusations of police brutality appeared in the news, Nick always pictured Bill Russell in some back room with a cowering suspect. But Bill, who had never married, also had a softer side as revealed by the tender care he took of his aged mother who shared his townhouse. This lady was known to be caustic, opinionated and outspoken, yet Bill never quavered under some of the more withering insults she hurled at him in public and always responded with patience and respect—a marked contrast from the edgy, stern demeanor he displayed to all others.

Nick, with no enthusiasm, opened the front door and quickly called out, "Christina, it's me and Bill Russell," for fear she might come scampering down the stairs in some scanty outfit much too provocative for this time of day, which was part of her great allure: the unexpected. But for his eyes only. Christina answered "Okay" from upstairs and did not appear. "I'll be up to help you in a few minutes," Nick extemporized, hoping to keep Bill's visit to a quick one.

Nick led Bill to the expansive family room in the back of the condo. "Would you like anything to drink?" he asked automatically and regretted the offer as possibly extending Bill's visit. Bill declined, and while Nick sat on the leather sofa, Bill remained standing, his eyebrows twitching like faulty elevator doors.

"Is there anyone else here?" Bill asked in a gravelly whisper as if he were about to do an electronic sweep of the premises. Since Nick's exchange with Christina had been at high decibels, he assumed Bill meant anyone besides the lady upstairs, so he said "No."

"You're sure?" Bill asked, still suspicious.

"I don't think so," Nick replied, bored, "unless there's a poltergeist lurking in the basement that we don't' know about."

Bill ignored Nick's comment and mocking smile.

"This is for your ears only," Bill said with such gravity that Nick thought he might be announcing his discovery of Jimmy Hoffa's body or, at the very least, coming out of the gay closet. Nick nodded and Bill continued. "I'm not sharing this with Helen because even though she's the Board president, as a woman she's too excitable."

*He **is** coming out of the closet*, Nick thought with mounting curiosity, while noting Bill's misogynistic remark.

"It's about Emma Craig's suicide," Bill intoned with all the solemnity of an archbishop but the diction of a taxi driver. "The detective on the case is an acquaintance of mine and he shared his doubts with me."

Bill paused, searching for Nick's reaction, but Nick met his stare with a neutral expression, not quite treating Bill as a reliable transmitter of another's opinion.

"He thinks Emma was much too frail to get up on a chair, fling the rope across the high beam in her living room, tie it securely and then kick the chair away."

Nick hadn't previously given any thought to the details of Emma Craig's suicide, but now, hearing the specific steps involved and recognizing Emma's frailties, he had to agree that it would seem to be extremely challenging, if not impossible, for her to have executed all those maneuvers.

"Well, he's got a point, " Nick acknowledged, half to himself, before playing the devil's advocate and adding, "but it's not entirely out of the realm of possibility that some heightened state of despair gave her extra strength."

"For Christ's sake, Nick," Bill thundered, "she was eighty-six and always used a walker, and the walker was found in her bedroom, at last twenty feet away from where she was hanging."

Nick had to mentally concede that this was a compelling fact supporting a theory of foul play. Still resisting any dreadful conclusions he said, "I admit that the absence of the walker could cause suspicion, but, again, it's not irrefutable proof in my mind of murder."

Having said the word "murder" out loud for the first time brought an involuntary grimace streaking across Nick's face. Bill, too, seemed to be encouraged by Nick's reference.

"How about the absence of any note?"

"I don't think all suicides leave notes," Nick offered in a less than-convincing tone.

"There's something else!" Bill bellowed with a triumphal gleam. "The knot used to tie both ends of the rope was a very complicated knot known only to expert seamen."

"Maybe Emma was in the Waves," Nick said facetiously but Bill shook his head. "Maybe the Girl Mariners," Nick stubbornly persisted but Bill was clearly losing patience. "No. And she came from Omaha and never seems to have been even near the ocean until she moved here to be near her only living child, her daughter, after her husband passed away."

"Maybe he was a seaman and taught her how to tie knots," Nick persisted. "Maybe he was in the Navy."

Bill waved his arms dismissively. "He was an insurance salesman and was 4F. Punctured eardrum."

Nick would not concede. "Maybe they sailed on some lake in Omaha, and both learned about seamen's knots"

Nick was taking devilish pleasure in annoying Bill with all these highly implausible explanations since he wanted Bill to storm out in angry frustration and leave him alone. He was thinking about the delectable Christina upstairs and not Emma Craig.

Bill paused and Nick watched the retired cop draw a massive intake of breath as his chest swelled before delivering his next piece of evidence. "There's one more thing: Emma was known to have severe arthritis in her hands. How the hell could anyone with that condition tie so intricate a knot?"

While Nick remained outwardly calm, refusing to join Bill's rush to judgment, inwardly little bells and whistles were going off. He responded with a practical question. "Was any of this shared with the daughter?"

'Yes, but she's in a state of shock about her mother's death—they weren't getting along lately—and can't cope with adding murder to her plate, so she won't listen to the evidence right now."

Pragmatic considerations were now taking center stage in Nick's mind. "Will the detective file a suspicious death report?"

Bill took two steps forward and was now towering directly over the sitting Nick, his voice rising to a higher pitch of intensity as his arms flailed the air, narrowing missing Nick's nose. "He already has! Now the local papers will pick it up and the shit will hit the fan! This community will go ballistic! You've got to do something!"

Nick heard Bill's dire warnings and felt his body sinking lower into the leather sofa. If any community could go completely ballistic, surely it was this one, he reflected. Under ordinary circumstances they were a Loony Tunes congregation of many hyper-hysterics. With this information, they'd collectively foam at the mouth and fly over the moon, babbling and screeching as though they were confronting the end of the world. Yet, he had to admit, this official rendering of a suspicious death was enough to upset any community, causing suspicion and disquiet.

Nick's grimace returned as he realized that with this news in the local paper, the Marsden Grove community would never be the same. As for Bill's admonishment that Nick had to do something, he could no sooner hold back an avalanche or quell a tsunami than turn the course of events that were about to happen

Another thought skittered across Nick's mind. Who could have possibly murdered Emma Craig? And why? Was there a killer in their midst? He raced through his mental file of the residents' faces, and, while certain physiognomies might suggest a callous indifference toward others or distorted attitudes of self-importance, not one could be singled out as a verifiable potential killer. Eccentrics, yes! Malcontents, definitely! Wing nuts, perhaps! But a cold-blooded killer? Hard to imagine.

Amidst his dark, bewildering thoughts, a silly line from a radio program that his father loved to recite, replete with melodramatic gestures and exaggerated intonations, when Nick was a boy, suddenly popped up: "Who knows what evil lurks in the hearts of men? The Shadow knows." If only he had that ability of The Shadow to see into men's souls and uncover a killer. Lacking that capacity, he reluctantly resigned himself to the firestorm that lay ahead.

8

For the rest of the afternoon Nick was in a pensive mood, reflecting on the details that Bill Russell had adduced to support the local detective's conclusion of suspicious death.

At first Nick argued with himself how everything could be explained away without reaching a conclusion of foul play. But each time he tried to picture Emma Craig's leaving her walker in the bedroom, hoisting herself on a chair in the middle of the living room, and all that business with the complicated knotting of the rope and hurling it up over the cross beam of the cathedral ceiling, his feasibility arguments exploded and he was more convinced that Emma could never have done all this by herself. Then his mind would bound forward to the all-consuming question: Who?

It had always amused him to recognize how much people in this community knew about one another. Gossip, rumor and vitriol circulated like air, greedily gulped by seniors with too much time on their hands and not enough to occupy themselves. Idle speculation could magically be transformed into accepted fact. A sly comment uttered in a low, confidential tone with a raised eyebrow and a conspiratorial smile could galvanize any listener to a verdict of guilty.

From the frequently observed liquor store deliveries to Ted and Amy Clark's townhouse, everyone just knew they were alcoholics, especially since they never entertained. Actually, Nick thought, *that's pretty concrete.* And the Moriaritys' constant battles could be heard by many neighbors, usually culminating in Susan Moriarity's final lash-out, "Drop dead, you bastard." Her husband Jack would invariably reply, "I'll outlive you, bitch!" No matter what the topic of their ferocious combat, the curtain came down with these repeated memorable lines and peace would once again, but only temporarily, descend on Marsden Grove.

It was common knowledge that Henry Cushman, a widower and reputed lecher, was sleeping with Violet Tomby, a widow, for too many seniors with sleeping disorders had spied Henry slithering between his unit and Violet's at pre-dawn hours. For their own personal reasons, during the daytime they pretended to be only nodding acquaintances, but no one was fooled.

Mabel Thomas was regarded as a notorious flirt or, in the parlance of some ladies of the community, a slut, who, in her acknowledged eagerness to snare husband number three—the previous two had divorced her—openly pursued any single man on the horizon, even George Trumble. Unfortunately, George, a retired electrician and bachelor, was known to frequently receive packages from Victoria's Secret, and, never having been seen with any woman, was clearly, according to community consensus, a pervert. Nick thought bemusedly that if Mabel and George ever hooked up, they could wear matching underwear.

Alice Kramer had quickly become "that pack-rat lady." On her moving-in day, which always had neighbors gleefully on alert to make preliminary, and often harsh, judgments on the new resident's style, class, personal habits and sanity, Alice had reportedly crammed endless amounts of furniture, cartons, bric-a-brac, mementoes, files, a mammoth Spanish colonial dining room set, a baby-grand piano, several bird cages minus any birds and numerous boxes of Depends into her small, two-bedroom townhouse. Neighbors now complained of musty smells emanating from said dwelling and circulated the story that things were piled to the ceiling, with only a narrow pathway between rooms. Except for her reputed hoarding proclivities, Nick always considered Alice to be a very sweet and pleasant lady.

Of course, Dagmar Neilson's monomaniacal obsession with saving the planet through conservation and recycling was, despite the worthiness of her cause, preached with such blunt aggressiveness and fiery condescension that she was universally abhorred and dismissed.

Then there was Vincent Zabridini, the retired chemistry teacher who had recently moved in with a huge collection of books and what neighbors took to be "strange pieces of lab equipment." A dour man with long, unkempt hair and thread-bare clothes who kept to himself and seldom was seen leaving his unit except to return with bags of groceries and what was speculated as being "strange paraphernalia," the gossips had a field day rumor-mongering what he was up to. Everything from a mad bomber— "he's eastern European, you know"—to another Dr. Frankenstein, was bruited about with more or less conviction. Nick thought that he'd probably be the first person that suspicious eyes would gravitate to when the news about Emma Craig hit the papers.

Late that afternoon Nick and Christina took Charley for a long walk. Christina sensed Nick's unusual, distracted mood and made light conversation that required small responses and little engagement. The ever-alert Charley also sensed his master's pensive demeanor and quietly trotted at Nick's side, only occasionally scampering away to investigate some scent or movement before hurrying back, his large black eyes gazing solicitously on Nick.

Later, Christina prepared sausage and peppers, a dish that Nick particularly liked, while he prepared a salad. They worked side by side in silence, ate dinner with little conversation and then watched a classic movie before going to bed.

Tonight, even their love-making seemed abstracted and singularly brief before a perfunctory "Good Night," as Nick rolled over and stared into the darkness, still consumed with glum thoughts, perplexing questions and grave concerns for what was to come. Awake until the wee hours, his troubled slumber was then abruptly terminated by the shrieking of the phone.

Swimming slowly up to semi-consciousness, Nick wearily lifted the receiver and heard Fran Walker's high nasal squeal. "Have you seen the paper?"

The clock on the bedside table registered 7:10. Nick dazedly answered "No."

Clearly excited, Fran's voice was roused to a shrill pitch that pierced Nick's eardrum to the center of his being. "It's official," she shouted, highlighting the despairing tone of her tinny whine—she sounded like a character in a Disney cartoon. "The headline reads 'Suspected Murder in Marsden Grove.' This is terrible! What are we going to do?"

Arriving at full consciousness, Nick heard this existential question with amusement. "There is very little we can do," was his laconic reply.

"What proof do they have of murder?" Fran shouted defensively.

Again a calm response from Nick. "Doesn't the headline say 'suspected'? That's a couple of grades below an outright claim. What does the article say?"

"Let me get my glasses," Fran said, followed by a long pause and the audible shuffling of the newspaper. In fast cadences underscored by irate sighs, Fran read the brief article. Details, such as those Bill Russell had cited to Nick, were not included; the gist was that the investigating detective, identified as Jonathan Grimes, had found sufficient evidence to suspect foul play which warranted further investigation.

Fran followed up her reading the article with, "We have to have a community meeting."

Nick shuddered. Fran was big on meetings, "to let people offer their opinions," she would always say, as though all residents were objective and rational, like some model United Nations forum in a high school civics class. But the cacophony of raging voices that assaulted the air at these meetings always left her surprised and shaken. Yet, like some insane, masochistic dunderhead, she clung to this course of action as an impulsive reaction to all problems, large or small, that came to the Board's attention, blithely asserting that it was the ideal democratic response.

"Let's not be too hasty," Nick cautioned, envisioning the three-ring circus that any community meeting at this time would become. Ignoring the disquieting details that Bill Russell had confidentially shared with him, he continued with a lie. "We don't know why the detective suspects foul play, so there's no information we could share with the residents at this time. And giving them an open forum to build on their suspicions and fears, with no additional facts, would only exacerbate the problem and could lead to mass hysteria. That's the last thing we want."

"You don't think mass hysteria won't erupt from reading this article?" Fran said, her voice quivering.

Nick replied calmly, "I'm sure people will be upset, but we could put out a notice to all residents stating that we recognize how upsetting this article is, but at this time we have no further information and will keep them posted on all developments."

"Should we hire private detectives?" Fran asked abruptly. "After all, the reputation of our community and our property values are at stake here."

"Let's wait until the local detectives finish their work. I'm sure they'll be willing to give you up-dates on their investigation as president of our Board."

A prolonged silence ensued before Fran said, "Well, Nick, they'll have to report to you as vice president. My sister is very ill. I got the call last night and I'm heading for Oregon tomorrow and don't know when I'll be back."

SHIT! Nick screamed to himself, not believing this sudden story about a sick sister and realizing that he'd have to carry this load forward by himself since the Major, Big Foot and Cat Lady would be no help, only trouble.

"I didn't know you had a sister in Oregon," he said slowly, not concealing his suspicions.

"Oh, yes," Fran averred quickly. "I haven't seen her in years. We were never very close, even as children, because she's eight years older, but now that she's really sick I feel an obligation to help since she's all alone."

Fran delivered this monologue in a soft, halting cadence, and Nick couldn't make up his mind if that was because she was making it up as she went along or because she was genuinely moved by her sister's plight. He could hear violins wailing in the background of this plaintive tale but realized that, true or false, he was still Johnny on the Spot. Steady strokes were starting to beat at the back of his skull, a harbinger of a serious headache.

"Where can I reach you?" he asked as resignation slowly crept over him. There was another long pause.

"Well, Nick, I'm sorry but I'd rather you didn't. With my sister being so sick, I expect I'll have to devote all my time to her. I leave you in full charge."

"Thanks a lot?" Nick exploded with all the sarcasm he could muster, convinced now that Fran was lying through her teeth to avoid all the trouble ahead. He could picture her on some cruise ship in the Caribbean, sipping exotic cocktails, carefree and happy, congratulating herself on her clever ruse, while he slogged through all the crap to come.

His resentment soared as satanic fantasies overtook him. *Maybe Fran's ship would be captured by Somali pirates—where the hell was Somalia anyway?—and Fran would be sold into slavery. Fat chance! Who'd pay for a septuagenarian with the body of a swizzle stick and the voice of a crocus?*

"Good luck, Nick," Fran said, sounding as casual as if she were sending a son into the finals of the tennis tournament at the local country club, and abruptly hung up.

Nick hurled the phone across the room where it landed with a loud thud. Charley leapt up from his assigned post outside the closed bedroom door where he had been sleeping peacefully, dreaming of chasing birds and rabbits, and began barking in confusion and concern.

"Whoa!" Christine shouted, her head emerging from under the covers. "Are we at war?"

"We will be very soon!" Nick replied glumly and reached for Christina's body as a momentary escape from all the hell he could imagine coming. But anxiety is not an aphrodisiac, and lust surrendered to worrisome projections. He had to content himself with being cradled in Christina's soothing arms, as dark thoughts flowed in every direction. A momentary distraction was offered by Charley's audible whimpering, announcing he was ready for his morning walk.

9

By late that afternoon, all of Nick's glum predictions had come true, and the uproar reverberating throughout Marsden Grove was at a virulent fever pitch. Shortly after Fran's notice of abdication, the phone had never stopped ringing. Nick was fervently wishing that the phone had never been invented—curses on you, Alexander Graham Bell!—and that everyone was using smoke signals, like the Indians, to circulate information. At least that would have slowed the incessant drumbeat of wild imaginings and mounting hysteria.

The first caller was Jane Curtis, the Cat Lady. "I'm sorry to bother you, Nick, but all my neighbors are calling me about the newspaper article and when I tried to reach Fran, I heard a new message on her machine that said, "Sorry, I'm away from home. For any condo business please call Nick Dalton."

Nick was grinding his teeth as he realized that the little coward had already made her escape.

Jane continued. "What are we going to do? Should we call a meeting?"

Jane, who was as silent at all public gatherings as one of her cats stalking a mouse, had obviously caught the meeting fever from Fran. Nick repeated what he had told Fran earlier: with nothing to report, a meeting was purposeless.

"But everyone seems really upset," Jane responded.

"Look, Jane," Nick said curtly, "I don't care if they're tearing their hair out and foaming at the mouth; a meeting right now would do nothing to mollify their anxiety. You're our Board secretary. Why don't you send out a brief notice to all owners saying we know nothing beyond what the article said but we'll keep them informed of any new developments?"

"Should I add something about be sure to lock your doors?"

Nick's temples were throbbing as his anger simmered and his mind raced to a sarcastic response. *Yeah*, he screamed to himself, *lock your doors and bar the windows and buy a guard dog and get a shotgun and hunker down*, waiting for some maniac to strike. Instead he said, "Just leave it at what I said, okay?"

"The Major is already asking for volunteers to patrol the grounds and stand guard through the night," Jane said quietly.

"Jesus Christ!" Nick exploded. "Is he nuts? He'll turn this place into a war zone before we even know anything further."

"I'm just the messenger, Nick," Jane said indignantly.

"Sorry," Nick quickly responded. "You get that message I suggested out to the residents and I'll deal with the Major."

Nick heard his call waiting signal and ended his conversation with Jane. The next caller was Dr. Carlton Wright, the retired psychologist and master of meandering confabulations, whom Nick secretly called Gaseous.

"Hey, Nick, Carlton here. I'm just calling to see if I could be of any help. I hear all hell is breaking loose over the newspaper article about Emma Craig, and Fran seems to be missing. That pretty much leaves you as head honcho in the hot seat."

If there was anyone whom Nick could picture as being of less help than Carlton Wright, he quickly decided it would only be the two other members of his private version of the Three Stooges: the Major and the Reverend Tom

Schneider, or, as he privately called them, Pompous and Pious. Carlton would probably dissertate *ad nauseam* on the complex profiles of a killer or man's inherent instinct for violence or the cultural triggers that prompted murder. Endless soliloquies that Nick did not need to add to the challenges he saw in the offing.

"Thanks, Carlton. I appreciate your offer but for the moment we've got the matter in hand."

"You're going to have to act fast to quell all the hysteria," Carlton warned. "I was just taking a walk and heard people saying they know who the killer is. The accusations are flying. Let me know if there's anything I can do. If you want to call a meeting, I could talk about the psychological tendencies to project feelings and motives on to others that have little basis in reality. That might put a damper on all these wild rumors."

Nick wondered why everyone was expressing the need for a meeting as somehow being a solution to the rapidly spreading turmoil throughout the community when he saw it as being the worst possible approach for diminishing the frenzied speculation. Then he almost chuckled as he thought that Carlton's typically dry, esoteric monologue might put most of the residents to sleep, which was one way of temporarily abating the mounting consternation.

"I'll keep that in mind," was Nick's neutral reply, followed by, "Sorry, Carlton, I have to go. There's someone pounding at my door."

Nick hung up and hurried to the front door. There stood the Major in full dress uniform.

"I'm organizing a patrol guard," he pompously announced, with all the gravity of General MacArthur's famous declaration, "I shall return."

Nick grabbed him by the jacket and yanked him into the foyer. The Major seemed stunned and cowed by Nick's physical aggressiveness. This was not the way to treat an officer performing his duty. He looked bewildered. Nick got right up in the Major's face and spoke in a low, intense voice.

"This isn't an army camp or a war zone, and you're not General Patton," he said, still firmly gripping the Major's jacket and peripherally noting how the shoulders were excessively padded. "If you don't go back home and stop all this military bullshit, I'm going to beat the crap out of you!"

The Major's eyes were swiveling as if they were caught in a pinball machine. "But the murder..." he sputtered. "People have to be protected...It's my duty."

Nick's eyes were blazing and his nose was within an inch of the Major's. "We don't know this was a murder and if it was, we'll get protection from the police. You're not turning this place into an armed compound." Nick shook the Major by his jacket, hard. "Is that understood?" He didn't wait for an answer but jerked the Major out the door and slammed it with barely controllable rage.

Nick knew that the Major's playing at soldiering pressed all Nick's buttons. Still, Nick cautioned himself that he would have to exercise more self-control for the onslaught of irrational, wack-a-do responses that were sure to come now from all sides. The curtain was going up on the Marsden Grove Ridiculous Players' performance of Murder and Condo-monium, his own invented word, and he was, by default, the director of either a farce or a melodrama, perhaps both, whose finale was still to be decided.

10

The rest of the day was a cacophony of bleating voices and angry demands, all laid at Nick's door, as he had predicted, by virtue of his position as Board vice president and the sudden retreat of Fran Walker. When residents weren't calling on the phone, they were knocking/pounding on his door. Strident voices were ringing though his home and his brain.

Charley, who felt it was his duty to alert Nick of any visitor with loud but friendly barking, was vigilant throughout the day, adding his voice to the ongoing din.

Christina volunteered for duty and answered the phone calls, parroting the statement that Nick had given to the Cat Lady for distribution to the community but adding her own soothing words to calm frazzled nerves. Nick manned the front door and applied his own public-relations method for downgrading the level of anxiety. To little avail, he sensed.

At mid-afternoon, Christina suddenly shouted, "Nick, look across the street!"

Following her direction, Nick saw a van emblazoned with the letters of a local television station and a young woman whom he recognized as Vienna Campos, an investigative reporter. She was interviewing Jessie Knowles, the one member of the Board whom Nick had not heard from. Ms. Campos was holding her microphone above her head in order to reach proximity to Jessie's mouth. He loomed over her like a sheltering tree, his stern facial expression conveying his self-conscious importance. Nick could only imagine what he was saying and groaned loudly.

"Should you go talk to her?" Christina asked softly.

Nick debated the question for a moment before answering, "No. Whatever Big Foot is telling her, I couldn't undo, and it would look stupid for Board members to be contradicting one another."

Nick felt that the lure of the spotlight would be too enticing for Jessie Knowles to resist and he would sensationalize Emma Craig's death with unsubstantiated assertions of his own. "He's probably telling her that he knows who the murderer is," Nick said, helplessly.

Two hours later Christina and Nick sat in the family room watching the local news. Sure enough, the lead story was the suspicious suicide at Marsden Grove. Vienna Campos, pretty and composed, was reporting while standing in front of the pool pavilion.

"An apparent suicide of Emma Craig, eighty-six, a resident at our local senior condo community, Marsden Grove, is presently being investigated, and concerns of foul play have been raised, according to another resident, Mr. Bill Russell, a retired New York City police officer who is familiar with the case. While Mr. Russell would say nothing on camera, he announced at the Annual Marsden Grove Homeowners Meeting that there might be contradictory evidence surrounding the death of Ms. Craig. Mr. Russell refused to give this reporter any specifics to back up his claim. The local police department declined to comment, saying the investigation was ongoing. We'll follow up on this story as more information becomes available but, in the meantime, tensions are high among the many resident seniors for their own safety under this threatening cloud of suspicion."

The camera cut to Alice Kramer, the pack-rat lady, looking disheveled and worried. "This is very upsetting," she said to the microphone Vienna was shoving in her face. "It's always been so peaceful here. Now this! I don't know what to believe. I was Emma's neighbor and I discovered her body. Who knows? Maybe her killer was still lurking in the house. I'm frightened."

The camera now cut to Jessie Knowles as Vienna asked, "As a member of Marsden Grove's Board of Managers, how is the community responding to these suspicions of foul play?"

Nick could feel his entire body stiffening as he waited for Big Foot's response

Jessie looked stern and dour as he stared directly into the camera, like some head of state addressing the United Nations, and said, "Until we know all the facts we cannot make a determination, but in the meantime the Board is advising all residents to take the utmost precautions."

"God dammit!" Nick screamed at the television, leaping from his chair and alarming Charley who had been dozing at his feet but now growled in confused alarm. "The Board said nothing of the kind! Where does Big Foot come off speaking for the Board?"

Nick fell silent again as the camera cut back to Vienna who assumed a grave look to dramatize her words. "Marsden Grove, a lovely, upscale senior community whose peaceful way of life has been suddenly disrupted with the tragedy of a resident's suicide. But now, everyone is asking, was it a suicide or was foul play involved? Within this tranquil community fear is growing and neighbor looks at neighbor with questions and newly aroused suspicions. We will follow this developing story. This is Vienna Campos, reporting from Marsden Grove."

"Great!" Nick exploded, turning off the television. "Jack the Ripper stalks Marsden Grove!"

"Nick, it's not as bad as all that," Christina said softly. "This day has been a torture for you and you need to get away."

"Maybe I should invent a dying sister in Oregon who needs my immediate help," Nick said in disgust.

"No, I wasn't thinking of anything like that," she said, trying to soothe his frazzled nerves, "although it did work for Fran. Maybe you could discover a long-lost dying cousin in Toledo."

They both laughed, breaking the tension, and Christina hugged Nick's arm. "How about we drive out to that great restaurant in Amagansett that you were telling me about last week—the one that you and Judy used to go to on special occasions?"

"You mean The Cooked Goose?"

"Yes, that's the one. We'll order a bottle of wine and sit outside and watch the waves roll in and have a great dinner and just relax."

The picture Christina was painting in her creamy voice had a calming effect on Nick. He half smiled.

"And then," she continued, her voice changing to a flirtatious tone, "you'll have some more wine since I'll be the designated driver, and I'll drive you to my house and take advantage of you."

Nick's half smile became a full smile. Softly, with almost a purr, Christina began to sing, "Forget your troubles, come on, get happy. We're gonna chase all your cares away. Sing Hallelujah, come on, get happy...."

Her singing was interrupted as a grateful Nick swept her into his arms. "Promise you'll take advantage of me?" he said, circling her lips for a landing.

"I promise," she whispered just before their lips locked.

11

Early the next morning Nick drove back to Marsden Grove, feeling revitalized and ready to face any mounting crises at his community.

The evening had gone exactly as Christina had outlined it, including the ardent lovemaking after a great dinner and a bottle of Malbec and after-dinner cognac. As the designated driver Christina had let Nick consume most of the spirits and he was light-headed on the drive to her house but not too far gone to incapacitate him for gymnastic sex. He woke with a mild headache that disappeared after a hot shower and Christina's home-made waffles. Now he was ready for action.

After walking Charley, he parked the car in front of the pool pavilion, grabbed his gym bag from the trunk and headed for the gym. The gym was housed in a corner of the pool house and consisted of three treadmills, three stationary bicycles, two stair-lifts and a universal Nautilus, all crowded into such a small space that anyone on any machine could converse with anyone else on any other machine without raising one's voice.

Despite the grossly inadequate number of machines when compared to the number of residents, many seniors preferred outdoor walking regimens, frequent golf outings, games of tennis or exercising in the outdoor pool—all during the spring-through-fall seasons—and some of the older residents eschewed all forms of exercise except playing cards, turning on the television and stumbling to the bathroom during the night. Consequently the tiny gym was never crowded, especially early in the morning when Nick preferred to use it.

He had a standard one-hour workout routine, using the four types of machines, three times a week, augmented by as many rounds of golf as he could arrange during the week with fellow residents or friends. His weekend golfing outings were always reserved for Christina who, even during the summer months, was either taking classes or teaching at a community college on weekdays.

Upon entering the gym Nick was greeted by Helen Parker, his usual workout companion at this early hour. Nick regarded Helen as a marvel. In her mid-eighties, her tall body was as compact and sinewy as a long-distance runner's, which, indeed, she was, when she wasn't swimming laps in the pool or performing a rigorous strength-building exercise on the universal Nautilus.

During their early-morning sessions over many months, Nick had learned that Helen had been a triathlon competitor in Poland before immigrating to America as a young woman in the nineteen-fifties. Shy and quiet, Helen mostly kept to herself. She had never married and had no family. Only with Nick's gentle urgings and friendly overtures did she open up and share a little of her history. Nick regarded her as one of the nicest people in Marsden Grove and looked forward to her company as they huffed and puffed through their workouts, exchanging only occasional comments and mostly relishing the silence and inward concentration on their routines.

No matter what the temperature or how strenuous her workout, Nick noticed that Helen always wore some long-sleeve type of shirt. When he casually remarked about this, she said it helped her to sweat more and burn up calories. Nick thought that if anyone did not need to burn up calories and lose weight, it was Helen. In contrast, he would always begin his workout with a T shirt or a tank top, only to shuck it half way through his routine. He greatly admired Helen's discipline and dedication to staying fit.

"Quite a bit of attention we're getting!" Nick remarked, crossing from a treadmill to a stationary bicycle, hoping to get Helen's response to all the hubbub about Emma Craig's death.

Moving rapidly on the stair-lift, Helen smiled slightly but said nothing.

"What do you think of all the fuss?" Nick asked pointedly.

Never slowing her rapid pace on the stair-lift, Helen responded, "Let's wait and see."

Nick persisted. "You're not frightened by all the talk of foul play?"

Helen seemed to be focusing on some far distant spot as her legs pumped in a fast rhythm. "Not really," was all she said. After a pause, she sent Nick a shy smile and laconically repeated, "Let's wait and see."

Nick was relieved to hear Helen's unemotional response and hoped that her reaction was mirrored by a good number of the more sensible residents of Marsden Grove, unaffected by the hysteria running rampantly among the hotheads and screamers.

Nick finished his workout and headed for the shower in the men's room. This one shower had been squeezed into the men's bathroom as an afterthought when residents complained about having only the outdoor shower next to the pool. It was a sad, makeshift affair, abutting the toilet on one side and the sink on the other, demarcated by a moldy shower curtain on three sides.

A rusted shower head delivered a paltry stream of water. If you bent down to wash your feet, your elbow invariably hit the toilet tank. If you leaned in the other direction, you hit the edge of the sink. Nick regarded it as a war zone, but he didn't want to get into his car all sweaty and smelly and drive back home, so he tolerated the humiliating contortions he had to perform to avoid bangs and bruises.

Clean, if not refreshed, Nick headed home and found a black sedan parked in his driveway with a man sitting in the driver's seat, smoking a cigarette. Nick pulled up in back of the sedan and as he got out of his car, so did the man, extinguishing his cigarette on the driveway with his foot, which annoyed Nick.

The two men walked toward each other. The stranger was about the same height and weight as Nick and wore a rumpled light-weight windbreaker, khaki slacks and open-collared shirt. His face had a weathered, craggy look and his full head of hair was dull gray. His dark eyes, even from a short distance, were piercing.

The man held an opened wallet chest-high, and a badge glinted in the morning sun. "Mr. Dalton?" was all he said and Nick said "Yes."

"Detective Grimes. I'd like to talk to you. Do you have a few minutes?" His voice was deep, his words delivered in a monotone, as if bored by their very utterance.

Nick nodded, responding quickly, "Come on in," and led the way past the foyer and back to the family room.

Charley, his tail wagging lazily, sniffed the detective.

"Hope you don't mind my dog," Nick said.

'Love dogs," the detective replied, scratching behind Charley's ears, much to the dog's obvious delight. "He probably smells my dog. She died of old age last week but her scent is still on my clothes. Their sense of smell is a hundred times more acute than ours."

"Sorry about your dog. I'm going to make some coffee. Would you like some?"

"If it's no bother, sure," the detective replied, still in a monotone as he surveyed the room with its adjoining open-style kitchen and large windows overlooking a small, tree-shaded patio. He pointed to a picture of Nick next to his helicopter in Vietnam. "Nam?" he asked and Nick nodded. "Me, too. One hell of a place!" Nick nodded in agreement and, as with most veterans of that unsalvageable, costly and inglorious war, a subtle bond of shared, nightmarish experience instantly formed between the two men.

Charley, deciding that all was right with his world, was too polite to pester the stranger for more ear scratching once he had stopped, so he retreated to his large cushion in the corner of the room and took a nap.

"What can I do for you, detective?" Nick asked casually as he busied himself preparing the coffee. "Have a seat, please."

Detective Grimes chose a chair next to the black leather sofa. Once seated, with his jacket opened, Nick saw a paunch that was larger than his own. He guessed the detective's age to be early sixties. *Probably just wants to get through the next few years with no fuss and retire*, he thought. He remembered that cops on Long

Island made good money and had good pension benefits.

Detective Grimes took out a small notepad and was flipping through the pages. "You're the vice president of the Board of Managers, right?" The monotone never changed.

"Yes," Nick said, waiting for the coffee to brew.

"And Mrs. Fran Walker is the president but she's not here. She's away."

"That's right, detective. A sick sister in Oregon is what she said."

Grimes raised his head from the notepad, having picked up the equivocal tone in Nick's last sentence.

"You don't believe that?" he asked quickly, his voice for the first time rising.

Nick hesitated for a moment before committing himself. "I suppose I do, yes."

"Suppose?" said the detective, his voice rising still further.

"Well, it just came out of the blue, you know. Suddenly, when the local newspaper ran that article about the investigation of Emma's death. At that time, frankly, I thought Fran wanted to escape all the questions and posturing from our more incendiary residents, but I don't think there was any deep, furtive motive behind her escape. I guess I was mad because I'd get all the shit kicked at my door in her absence.

"Did you?" The voice was now down in pitch.

"Pretty much, yesterday."

The detective switched topics. "Are you and Bill Russell friends?"

Nick busied himself with pouring coffee into two cups as he weighed his response. "Not really. I know him, of course, as a member of our community but we're not friends."

Glancing again at his notepad, Grimes said, "It was Bill who started a ruckus at your annual meeting by saying there were suspicious circumstances surrounding the death of Emma Craig. Is that correct?"

"Yes, Bill said he had gotten his information from the detective on the case. I guess that's you He said you and he were friends."

"Hardly!" Grimes shot back. Now his voice took on a definite overtone of annoyance. "He was hanging around the station and we knew he was a retired cop from the city and he asked me some questions which, as a courtesy to a fellow-officer, I answered.

"I see," was all Nick could think of in response. "Cream? Sugar?" he asked, holding a cup up.

"Black," Grimes responded before asking the question Nick had been anticipating. "Did Russell share any details with you?"

Nick placed the coffee cup on the side table next to Grimes' chair and sat down on the sofa, all the while deciding how to answer. He gave himself a few extra seconds by sipping his coffee before replying. In those few seconds he decided that honesty was required when dealing with the law.

"Yes, he did. He wanted me to realize what a serious challenge we could be facing if it turned out that foul play was involved."

"Did he believe it was?" Grimes asked, his dark eyes focused like laser beams on Nick.

"Yes, he did. And I have to add that he convinced me that there were enough nagging little discrepancies about the suicide to be suspicious."

"So much for professional confidentiality!" Grimes said with clear annoyance. 'Have you shared any of these details with anyone else?"

"No," Nick said emphatically.

Grimes consulted his notepad. "You live alone?"

"Only part-time," Nick said with a slight smile. "My girlfriend has her own home and she stays here mostly on weekends."

"And you didn't share any of the information that Russell told you with her?"

Again, Nick offered an emphatic "No," grateful that, out of consideration for Christina, he had spared her these troubling details.

"Okay," Grimes said, reaching for his coffee and taking a big gulp. "You're in the loop now, whether you want to be or not, so I'll have to trust you, which is more than I can say for Russell. He's out of the loop, understood?"

Nick felt an unexpected surge of pride and said, "Completely!" He was now officially ordained a crime fighter or, at least, a confidant of crime fighters. He flashed back to his childhood with his Dick Tracy badge and his imitation two-way-radio wrist watch.

"Tell me what you know about Emma Craig!" Grimes said peremptorily, flipping to a clean page in his notepad.

Nick took another sip of his coffee, suddenly feeling very relaxed.

"I didn't know her very well, but Emma was universally regarded as one of the sweetest ladies in our community. Everybody loved her.

Every time I saw her, she was always smiling, always upbeat, you know." Nick paused before adding, "Yet I always had a strange feeling that behind the smiles and her sunny disposition lay some dark shadows. There were just moments when I thought her eyes revealed a sadness that didn't match her sunny exterior. Just some crazy intuitive feeling. I suppose I shouldn't even mention it."

Detective Grimes made a notation in his notepad before remarking, "You'd be surprised how often we go by gut feelings or our intuitive responses in solving cases." Then he asked, "No known hostilities between her and any other residents?"

"None that I know of. I can't imagine anyone being mad at Emma. She was that good-natured." Then Nick thought of something Bill Russell had told him. "Bill told me she wasn't getting along with her daughter, but just who was mad at whom I have no idea."

Grimes flipped his notepad and then said, "The daughter was angry at her mother because Emma was becoming frail and the daughter thought she should leave Marsden Grove and move to an assisted living facility or a nursing home. But Emma loved it here and she refused.

The daughter didn't want to force her but she was mad and stopped coming to see her mother, thinking this might influence her to change her mind. She called Emma occasionally and felt her mother was depressed over not seeing her but still would not consent to move."

"You know, detective…" Nick began before being interrupted.

"Call me Jonathan."

"Okay. And I'm Nick. You know, Jonathan, the seniors here form some tight bonds with other residents. We have a ninety-five-year-old gentleman who's been ailing for some time and is being taken care of by three of his immediate neighbors who won't hear of him going to a nursing home at this point in his life."

"Who were Emma's friends?"

"I really don't know who her close friends were. I'd see her often in the card room playing bridge with a group of ladies, but how close they were to her I can't say. I suppose her neighbors could answer that question. Or maybe her daughter."

"The daughter's changed her tune," Jonathan said, closing his notepad and rising from his chair. "Once she read the newspaper article and saw the local news report last night, she called me this morning, crying and screaming that her mother had been murdered, but she had no idea who might have done it."

Nick stood up. "Jonathan, given all those details about the walker in the bedroom, the complicated knots, no suicide note and Emma's lack of physical strength to accomplish how she died, isn't it still possible that she could have summoned all her strength in a pronounced state of depression to take her own life?"

Jonathan's piercing stare made Nick falter. "Honestly?" the detective asked gravely.

Nick nodded.

"While anything's possible, in my professional opinion: No. But right now we have no witnesses, no suspects and no incriminating evidence pointing to anyone. Only these contradictory details that definitely arouse suspicion. The crime lab came back with nothing. I checked with her doctors and there was no sudden onslaught of some serious illness, so that motive's been eliminated. Right now, we're at the starting gate with only a hunch to go on."

Jonathan and Nick shook hands, and Jonathan handed Nick his card. "That's my private line. Call me if you hear anything. Thanks for your time and the coffee. I'll be in touch." He turned to walk toward the door, then stopped, turned around and gave Nick another penetrating look. "In the meantime...," he said, putting two fingers to his lips, "say absolutely nothing!"

"Mum's the word!" Nick said and immediately felt ridiculous for uttering such a banal, juvenile expression. "Yes, I understand," he added as the detective closed the door behind him, leaving Nick in a tumult of jarring, dangerous thoughts about what might happen next.

He wanted to clear his mind and reached for Charley's leash. The dog, instantly aroused from his snoozing, leaped up from his cushion and scampered to Nick's side, eager for an excursion. "Let's take a nice, long walk, Charley," Nick said, and the dog's enthusiastic tail wagging showed he understood and agreed.

12

The easy pattern of Nick's relationship with Christina had fallen into place without forethought or planning. Monday night she developed lesson plans either for her elementary students during the school year or for her community college course during the summer. Thursday night she tutored a special-needs child of whom she was very fond.

Wednesday was Nick's poker night with a group of men including his friend George Perkins, who got him started on internet dating that, after many disappointments, had led to discovering Christina; the psychologist Carlton Wright who mercifully didn't spout theories on the psychological dynamics of winners and losers and in this setting was bearable; and Jack Moriarity who was happy to escape from battling with his wife Susan for one night.

That left Tuesday, Friday and the weekend for dates, togetherness, golf and lots of lovemaking. Neither resented the time spent in the company of others; those absences just seemed to sweeten the anticipation of their reunions.

The next Wednesday the poker players had no sooner assembled when George Perkins, who was not a Marsden Grove resident but had read the newspaper article, started kidding about the Emma Craig case. "So why did you do the old lady in, Nick?" he asked with obvious glee. "Was she two-timing you with Carlton?" George poked Carlton's shoulder.

Jack Moriarity entered the japing contest. "Nick likes them old and frail so they can't get away that easily."

Now it was Carlton's turn. "Yes, but once he got Emma cornered in the bedroom, she got so scared, she rushed into the living room without her walker and hanged herself."

Nick had been taking this ribbing with a good-natured smile, but now his smile froze. "What did you say?"

Carlton momentarily looked confused by Nick's sudden, intense expression, but then he repeated what he had just said.

Alarms were ringing in Nick's head. How did Carlton know about Emma's walker being in the bedroom when she hanged herself in the living room? Should he challenge Carlton here and now? Should he say nothing and report this incident to Jonathan tomorrow morning? He weighed both courses of action and decided it would be better to tell Jonathan and let him follow up on it. For the rest of the night he was noticeably distracted as wild scenarios played out in his mind, and he lost heavily.

The next morning he reached Jonathan on his private line and recounted what Carlton had said

"Thanks. I'll follow up on this."

That afternoon Jonathan called back. "A dead end! Loose-lips Russell told him about the walker."

"Did Russell admit it?"

"Yeah. I cornered him and he sputtered and stammered but finally admitted it."

"Do you think he told anyone else?"

"He swears that only you and this Carlton Wright got any information from him. Did you know they were friends?"

"No, but they live next door to each other and that can explain it. "

"Now we've got three residents in the loop: you, Wright and, of course, Russell. I had to tell Wright about your reporting his comment to me."

"Carlton's a professional: he knows how to keep secrets."

"Then why did he mention the walker at your poker game?"

Nick thought for a minute before responding. "Maybe he thought it was common knowledge that Russell had mentioned to others. I'll tell Carlton to keep that information to himself."

"I've already done that. Thanks again, Nick. Keep your eyes and ears open."

"Sure thing," Nick responded, and the phone conversation ended.

A short time later Nick's bell rang and it was Carlton. Invited in, Carlton started talking immediately.

"I spoke with Detective Grimes this morning and I'm sorry about last night, Nick. Bill Russell shared with me the odd details surrounding Emma's death. He wanted my opinion about possible foul play."

"And what did you tell him?"

"I said the most compelling evidence was the lack of a suicide note. The overwhelming majority of suicides leave a note and that's especially true among the elderly."

"Any idea who might have had it in for Emma?" Nick asked.

"God, no! The detective asked me the same thing. She was a gentle, sweet lady and everybody seemed to like her. Even the crazies around here! But, you know, Nick, the usual suspects are the people closest to the victim and you never know what's going on within a family circle."

"You think the daughter could have killed her own mother?" Nick asked, dubiously.

"I'm just saying that no one should be beyond the bounds of suspicion. We don't know what went on between them."

"We know that the daughter brought Emma here to Marsden Grove so she could be near her. We know that the daughter seemed to be solicitous of her mother's welfare and wanted her to have more care by moving into an assisted living facility."

Nick paused as he thought back to what Bill Russell had mentioned about the daughter's admitting to Jonathan that she and her mother were temporarily estranged because of Emma's adamant refusal to move.

Carlton said, "You never know the underlying feelings between seemingly close and loving relatives, is all I'm saying. Believe, me, what I've discovered in working professionally with families would curl your hair. Rampant hostility and murderous thoughts are not uncommon."

Nick was quick to respond. "But how many people act on those murderous thoughts?"

"Fortunately for society, very few. That's why they seek help. But there's always a few..."

Carlton's voice took on the monotone of one of his pedantic lectures, causing Nick's mind to stray to unsettling questions and possibilities that he could not fathom but that definitely revolted him.

"Has Grimes said anything about the daughter?" Carlton's question interrupted Nick's thoughts.

"No," Nick answered, "but I'm sure he's looking at everything. It just seems to be like searching for that proverbial needle in the haystack."

"Well, even if the daughter is innocent, she's the only one who can provide information about Emma's life and history that might give us something to go on."

"Us!" Nick asked, his eyebrows rising.

Carlton smiled. "You and I and Bill Russell seem to be privy to the case now, and I know I'm willing to help in any way I can."

Nick had a fleeting thought that Carlton would love to have a Dick Tracy badge and a two-way radio wrist watch as he played at being a detective.

"You can leave Bill Russell out of it," Nick said. "Detective Grimes is really angry about Bill's loose lips. I wouldn't overstep my bounds here, Carlton. If we're needed, we'll be called. In the meantime, we should say nothing to anyone about what we know. Understood?"

"Yes, of course," Carlton said sheepishly and then added in a conspiratorial tone, "Let's keep in touch."

Nick thought Carlton might suggest their having a code word and a secret signal. All this playacting had gone far enough.

"I've got to make some calls," Nick said abruptly and showed Carlton to the door. He was brewing some coffee when the doorbell rang and Nick found Gillie at his doorstep.

Gillie had been the general handyman at Marsden Grove since it opened ten years ago. He was a Jack-of-all-trades and a hard worker, but he had a drinking problem that every now and then got out of hand and interfered with his work. As soon as Nick opened the door he could see that this was one of those times.

Gillie, short and heavily muscled, with thick black hair that started about an inch above his thick black eyebrows, was about fifty. Nick had always liked Gillie and respected his work ethic. Gillie's wife had left him and gone back to Romania with their only child and Nick felt that Gillie had good cause for drinking but kept that opinion to himself.

"What's up, Gillie?" Nick said cheerfully as Gillie swayed slightly and, in his heavily accented, truncated English, said, "Like to tell you something."

Nick led Gillie to the family room where Gillie stood, still swaying slightly as his eyes lurched nervously about the room. "I see someone leave lady's house on morning she die," he said, catching Nick by surprise.

Nick cocked one eyebrow. "Was it her neighbor, Alice Kramer?" he asked, knowing that Alice had discovered Emma Craig's body.

"No. Other person," Gillie said.

"Who?"

"Don't know. I just come to work and was still pretty dark, but I see person, all in black, black pants, black jacket with hood covering most of face."

"Man or woman?"

"Don't know. Tall, thin: could be man, could be woman."

"Have you told this to Detective Grimes?"

Gillie's expression darkened. "No. I not want trouble." Now he swallowed hard and his Adam's apple did a little jig. "Then I think maybe this important."

"Yes, it certainly could be important," Nick said, recognizing that an unidentified person leaving Emma's townhouse on the morning of her suspicious death would support the theory of foul play, at least until that person was identified and his or her presence otherwise explained. "I'm sure the detective will want to speak to you."

Nick could see the frightened look in Gillie's eyes but attributed it to general nervousness that many foreigners had in making contact with law enforcement officials, based on bullying or mistreatment by police in other countries. Nick now understood why Gillie had fortified himself with his drink of choice, whatever that was, before coming forward with his important news.

"I know you're busy so why don't I report what you've told me to the detective?" Nick said, happy to allay Gillie's apprehension by interceding for him. Gillie broke out in a smile of sheer relief at Nick's offer.

After Gillie left, Nick weighed this new information, finding that all the unfolding details pointed conclusively to murder. And the questions of who and why immediately arose.

Once again, he felt the need to clear his mind. Calling for Charley who came bounding to him, he leashed the happy dog and headed for a trail in the next-door Preserve. They walked the trail for over an hour, which clearly refreshed Charley but left Nick unable to escape ominous thoughts.

13

Nick had a deep desire to share everything about this unfolding mess with Christina but honored his promise to Jonathan, as frustrating as that promise was turning out to be. Given the unctuous seriousness with which Carlton Wright took his position of "being in the loop," Nick felt reluctant to add to Carlton's inflated sense of importance. Concluding that his only release might come from chatting with Jonathan, he called the detective on his private line.

Jonathan picked up on the second ring with a terse "Grimes here."

"Oh, I thought you might be away from your desk," Nick lamely proclaimed.

"I am. This is my cell number. What's up?"

"I don't know if you've spoken to Gillie, our general handyman, but he told me he saw someone leaving Emma Craig's townhouse early in the morning on the day of her death."

"I spoke to him briefly and he didn't mention anything like that to me," Jonathan said briskly.

"Gillie's from Romania and I think he's scared of police and scared of getting involved. His conscience seems to have gotten the best of him, but he fortified himself generously with liquor before blurting out his news to me."

"Has he mentioned this to anyone else?"

"I didn't think to ask him. Sorry. But I'd bet that because of his anxiety about being involved, he only told me."

"Approximately what time did he see this person?"

Nick thought for a moment. "Well, Gillie comes to work before six and he said it was still pretty dark, so it must have been shortly after he arrived."

"That's around the time we placed the death," Jonathan said. "It fits. Okay, I'll follow up."

There was a pause and Nick expected Jonathan to hang up without further ceremony, but then Jonathan said, "Did you know Emma had a sister?"

"No," Nick replied.

"She had legally changed her name from Strelitz to Steele not too long after immigrating to this country with her family. She was killed in a hit-and-run about five years ago in Bucks County. They never caught the driver."

"That's in Pennsylvania, isn't it?" Nick asked.

"Yeah," Jonathan responded, then paused again before adding, "The police found a strange note in the sister's home, threatening to expose some terrible secret in her past if she didn't meet the writer at a designated time and place not far from where she lived. The note was dated the day she was killed. Evidently she was on her way to meet the writer when she was hit."

"And no one saw her get hit?"

"No. It was late at night and she was crossing a not-very-heavily-trafficked street, even in the daytime."

"Was someone trying to blackmail her?"

"Could be, but the note didn't mention that— just said to meet. Maybe the writer didn't want to incriminate himself with a written threat of blackmail."

"What do you make of this?" Nick asked, his mind searching for parallels in the death of Emma's newly discovered sister.

"Well, it's curious that Emma's sister died under circumstances that, because of the note, could indicate foul play; or it just could have been a coincidence that she was on her way to meet the writer of the note and was very anxious, not paying attention, and some random car accidentally hit her and, seeing that no one was a witness, decided to speed off."

Nick was digesting all this startling new information when Jonathan added, "It was Emma who was discovered as the only relative, and she claimed the body. According to her friends and neighbors at Marsden Grove who spoke to me, Emma never mentioned having a sister."

"No, I never heard of any relative except for her daughter." Nick said, adding, "But I wasn't very close to Emma."

"I asked her daughter about her mother's sister, and she claimed she never heard of any sister and knew nothing about her."

"That's curious," Nick offered.

"Yeah, but maybe there was some long-standing feud between the two sisters and they hadn't communicated since leaving Germany as young girls. The local police report said the only way they discovered Emma's existence was because of a small insurance policy to cover burial expenses, with Emma listed as the beneficiary."

"Do you believe the daughter?" Nick asked, trying to fit this new piece into the scrambled puzzle.

"Don't know yet," Jonathan replied, obviously trying to codify the puzzle himself, which made Nick feel less stupid. "Thanks for the news about Gillie. I'll follow up."

"Please try to reassure him that he's not in any trouble," Nick offered quickly.

"I've been doing this work for a hell of a long time, Nick, and I think by now I know how to approach people and put them at ease. That's how we get most of our important information—when they're so relaxed, they blurt things out."

Nick could almost hear a rippling chuckle behind Jonathan's words. "Okay, I get it," he said in a chastened tone.

"By the way, Nick," Jonathan continued. "I'm taking you into my confidence because I'm hoping you'll be my eyes and ears in the community, but don't mention anything to anyone else."

"Not even to Dr. Wright? You told him he was in the loop."

Jonathan replied quickly. "I said that because he might be helpful in analyzing behavioral patterns or providing general psychological profiles, since our expert in these matters is on a leave of absence, but there's no need to tell him everything. He's a bit of a windbag."

"I understand," Nick said before hearing the click at the other end.

Nick fixed himself a sandwich and sat on the leather sofa in the family room. Charley settled by Nick's feet, looking with heightened anticipation at each bite Nick took because Charley knew the ritual of Nick's saving the last morsel for him.

Much to Charley's disappointment the phone rang, interrupting Nick's progress to the last bit for Charley. The disappointment in Charley's eyes was visible to Nick who, still holding the partially eaten sandwich, answered the phone. Charley made a little whimper of discouragement and put his head on his paws in a definite pout.

As soon as Nick heard the voice at the other end, he, too, assumed a pouting expression because Sonia Arcadivich was the last person he wanted to hear from just now. He regarded Sonia as the biggest kook in the whole community, the standard by which all other kooks could be judged and found wanting.

Sonia spoke with a thick Russian accent and was revered by the other kooks as a spiritualist or a mystic or a fortune teller, depending on what hat Sonia was wearing when she went into some trance-like state and assumed another occult personality. So extravagant were Sonia's claims to see into the future that she could tell anyone's fortune through interpreting the stars' conjunction, tea leaves, coffee grounds or even soap stains at the bottom of your sink. Or she could just stare intensely into your eyes and "see your soul."

Sonia celebrated her having descended from a long line of seers, living deep in the Ural Mountains, and she dressed as though she were still living with her tribe: long dark skirts, chunky boots, peasant blouses and lots of oversized jewelry that she identified as powerful amulets and sold to other residents at astronomical prices. The only American aspect of Sonia's life was her having married and buried three American husbands. Obviously, she hadn't seen too clearly into their future or perhaps she had! Her age was anywhere from sixty to one hundred, as her face was hidden under heavy makeup.

Sonia, when not reading palms, tea leaves or the random arrangement of bubble gum wrappers, was busy casting astrological charts for a surprising number of residents who would barely get out of bed without consulting her. From what Nick had heard through the grapevine, Sonia charged hefty fees for her arcane services and invariably warned her clients to beware of falling. Given the general age category of the community and the eyesight and balancing problems many residents faced, this warning was sure to be fulfilled at some point, enhancing Sonia's *bona fides* in predicting the future.

Now here she was, calling Nick, and he could make an accurate prediction about what she might say. With no preamble, she began.

"Nick, you must listen!" This was said in her deep, guttural voice. "Very bad spirits are hovering all around us."

Nick almost snickered as he thought Sonia's line could be the first sentence in a supernatural novel.

"When you say 'us,' Sonia, do you mean you and me?" Nick asked, trying to conceal his amused contempt.

"I have very bad feeling about the community."

Nick was tempted to reply with "Take two aspirin and call me in the morning," but he suppressed this temptation. Instead he asked, "Are the stars aligned against us?"

Sonia's voice sank deeper. "All signs point to some disaster."

"Maybe we should move," he suggested. "Do the tea leaves tell you that?"

"Very bad aura surrounding us. Bad news will come," Sonia said in *basso profundo*.

"Can you be more specific?" he challenged, knowing such a broad prediction could be smugly made in a community of seniors where someone was bound to fall or have a minor fender bender or lose a relative. Hell, even if a sink got clogged or a toilet backed up, Sonia could be covered. "Do you see the Apocalypse as imminent, or a tornado, or maybe a downward spiral in the stock market?"

"I see danger," Sonia intoned, refusing to be trapped into particulars. "We must beware!"

Nick was tired of this hocus-pocus. "Thanks for the heads-up, Sonia," he said brusquely and hung up.

He returned to eating his sandwich as Charley assumed a more alert stance at Nick's feet, once again anticipating his morsel. As much as he considered Sonia a complete charlatan, he had to laugh because he agreed with her about the dark uncertainty surrounding Emma Craig's death and the tumult that would erupt among all the seniors once all the facts were known.

Nick's thoughts flashed back to an incident about a year ago when a large pink flamingo ornament had been stolen from a resident's patio. After much gossip and swelling of facts, group hysteria had set in, convincing the more excitable residents that burglaries were rampant and no one was safe in his/her bed. Universal anxiety subsided only after the owner of the pink flamingo received a note from Dagmar Neilson, a one-woman committee on standards of good taste, saying that she had taken the statue and thrown it in the trash because it blighted the refined appearance of the community. Dagmar also enclosed a check to replace the "excrescence" with something more suitable for Marsden Grove's upscale reputation. The Board had been obliged to send Dagmar a cautionary note that threatened to call the police if any such arbitrary actions on her part occurred again.

If the disappearance of a pink flamingo could cause such a commotion, Nick could easily imagine the cataclysmic response to the murder of a resident. He was so completely lost in his somber thoughts that he forget to save the last bit of sandwich for Charley. He felt a paw gently tapping his leg and realized his omission from Charley's hurt expression.

"I'm sorry, Charley," Nick said. He got up and moved to the kitchen where he retrieved a dog biscuit from a bag in the pantry and offered it to Charley. Charley sniffed the biscuit, decided that while it wasn't as tasty or as meaningful as sharing his master's sandwich, beggars couldn't be choosers. He took the biscuit and swallowed it after two bites. Now he'd probably have to wait until dinner time when, after finishing his dinner, Nick usually offered his plate for Charley to lick before depositing it in the dishwasher. That routine was always a highlight of Charley's day. For now, however, sensing his master's pensive mood, he decided to take a nap and withdrew to his special cushion in the family room.

While Charley snoozed, Nick stewed.

14

Nick's pensiveness, as correctly perceived by the ever observant Charley, was due not only to the mounting mysteries of Emma Craig's death but also to his anticipating, not with pleasure, another community gathering on Saturday: the memorial service for Emma. He feared that despite the solemnity of the occasion, all hell could break loose among the lunatic fringe, the alarmists and the always-anxious. In his role as acting head of the Board, thanks to Fran Walker's decamping for parts unknown, he would certainly be in the thick of it.

Right now, however, he had an important call to make. He had checked the Board's master list of phone numbers for the relatives of residents to contact in any emergency and found Emma's daughter, Rosemary Craig, and her number. He dialed it. On the third ring he heard a thin, tired voice say "Hello."

"Hi, Miss Craig," Nick said, trying to combine both a solemn and upbeat tone and feeling as though he sounded like a recorded message. He rushed on. "This is Nick Dalton from Marsden Grove's Board of Managers. We'll all very sorry about your mother and we've scheduled a memorial service to honor her this coming Saturday and hope it's convenient for you to attend. Your mother was dearly loved and respected."

He was about to say something else when the voice on the other end exploded. "And will my mother's killer be there?"

"Excuse me?" Nick said, taken totally by surprise with this heated question.

"Don't pretend you don't know, Mr. Dalton, that my mother didn't commit suicide. She was murdered! And you want to have a memorial service so the killer can come and gloat?"

Ignoring the mounting evidence, Nick equivocated. "We can't say for sure that your mother was murdered. We only have some contradictory evidence," he offered feebly.

Rosemary Craig's voice increased in pitch and pace. "Well, here's some more contradictory evidence, as you call it, that I discovered yesterday while going through my mother's things and immediately gave to Detective Grimes. It's a note addressed to my mother and do you know what it said?"

This seemed like an odd moment to be playing twenty questions, so Nick remained silent without hazarding a guess.

Rosemary continued. "It said, 'You must pay for past sins.'"

Nick flashed back to Jonathan's reporting a similar note having been sent to Emma's sister in Pennsylvania before she died, but he made no mention of this. "That's certainly incriminating," he conceded, "but let Detective Grimes do his work and let us, as your mother's friends and neighbors, honor her. Can you come?"

A long pause before Rosemary answered. "You're a gated community with a guard at the entrance throughout the night, right?"

"Yes," Nick answered, having no idea where this unexpected question was leading.

"And did your guard report any stranger seeking entrance in the hours before my mother's death?"

"No," Nick said passively.

"And there was no evidence of a forced entry into my mother's townhouse, according to Detective Grimes, right?"

"Right," Nick responded, feeling as if he was on a witness stand testifying at a murder trial, being grilled by a sharp, aggressive lawyer.

Rosemary's voice now rose again. "Then that indicates to me that my mother was killed by someone in the community. Someone she knew and trusted. And until they find that murderer, no, Mr. Dalton, I want nothing to do with Marsden Grove or your memorial service!"

Nick was about to offer a feeble entreaty, but before he could utter a word, Rosemary continued with more heat. "And here's a news flash for you! The newspaper spoke of suspicious details. Well, I'm going to the newspaper office today and stating flatly that this **was** murder! Let's see how that affects the attractiveness of Marsden Grove to prospective buyers!"

Before Nick could remonstrate, the line went dead. Stunned by Rosemary's unrestrained fury, he suddenly remembered what Carlton Wright, the psychologist, had said about the closest family members not being above suspicion in murder cases. Jonathan, too, had said that everyone was a suspect. Throughout this torrid phone conversation, Nick reflected, Rosemary displayed only anger and aggression, with no crying, no indication of a great sense of loss, no inconsolable grief. Nick though of the old saying, "The best defense is a good offense," and began to entertain serious doubts about Rosemary's innocence.

In a thoroughly agitated state Nick turned to the one person he could share his thoughts with and dialed Jonathan's cell phone number. Even the laconic "Yeah" somehow seemed reassuring.

"I just got off the phone with a very angry Rosemary Craig," Nick blurted in rapid succession. "She won't attend our planned memorial service for her mother and is going to the local newspaper today to state unequivocally that she knows her mother was murdered. She says she found a note among her mother's things, threatening Emma, and she handed it over to you"

Nick was nearly breathless when he finished his summary report and waited expectantly for Jonathan's reply.

"Yeah, I have the note. It's similar to the one Emma's sister got. We can't stop her from going to the newspaper."

Nick asked his big question. "With all her aggressive anger, could this be to shield herself from suspicion?"

"Could be," Jonathan replied in his even, unemotional voice, "but one thing doesn't add up."

"What's that?"

"Gillie's description of the person he saw leaving Emma's home around the time she was murdered. I just finished speaking with him."

"How so?" Nick asked, confused

"Gillie specifically described the man or woman he saw as being tall and slim. Have you met Rosemary Craig?

"No."

"She's about five feet tall and a butter ball, so that leaves her out."

"Unless she was wearing stilts and several miracle girdles!" Nick chirped. Jonathan didn't laugh. "So we're still at square one," Nick added in a more serious tone.

"Afraid so," Jonathan replied. "My hunch is we have to connect the dots between Emma and her sister and whatever happened in the past. I'm working on that."

Nick remembered another part of his phone conversation with Emma's daughter. "Rosemary mentioned our all-night security system, which led her to feel confident that the murderer was from the community. Do you buy that?"

"Pretty much, but it wouldn't be impossible for someone intent on murdering a resident to find a way onto the property without being detected."

"But there could be some connection between Emma, her sister and someone in the community—some connection from the past, right?"

"Yeah, but just about anything's possible at this point," Jonathan said, before adding "Gotta go!"

Before Jonathan could hang up, Nick asked, "Will you be at the memorial service this Saturday?"

"I can't be there for the first part but I'll try to get there as soon as I can. Meantime, Nick, you're my eyes and ears, so be alert!"

Even with Jonathan's equivocal affirmation of what Nick had just posed, theoretically, about past connections, they were no nearer to solving the murder. Nick realized that he was now saying "murder" with total conviction, and that the consequences of this fact for the community could be devastating.

15

Each time a resident passed away, either in the community or after being removed to a nearby nursing facility, a memorial service was held at Marsden Grove. The idea for this practice came from Reverend Tom Schneider, the bombastic windbag that Nick had sarcastically nicknamed Reverend Pious.

"We need a formal closure to allow everyone to heal," the Reverend had explained. Nick felt that the Reverend just wanted opportunities to be center stage and practice his boring sermonizing skills again.

The memorial service for Emma Craig, given all the controversy surrounding her death and the rumors electrifying the community, thanks to the newspaper article and television reporting, was bound to be a three-ring circus with full attendance divided between those who wanted to light verbal fireworks and those who delighted in seeing the fireworks go off. There were also those residents who truly wanted to honor

Emma's life, but they would be caught in the emotional maelstrom.

Anticipating an overflowing crowd, Nick had ordered another canvas cover to shelter the seniors from the burning August rays. Sure enough, half an hour before the memorial service was scheduled to begin, almost every seat under the canvas top was taken and excited expressions on many faces bore evidence to the anticipated drama that might emerge. Clusters of residents were engaged in animated conversations. In surveying the swelling, excited crowd, Nick thought the only thing missing were vendors selling hot dogs and cotton candy and bookies taking bets on who Emma's murderer might turn out to be.

Nick noticed Sonia Arcadivich standing outside the canvas top, giving an electrifying performance to a surrounding group of devotees. By the sweep of her arms and her grim look and flashing eyes, Nick concluded she was forecasting either the end of the world or that Marsden Grove was besieged by a maniacal killer who would claim many more lives. The eyes of her rapt audience seemed to be bulging out of their sockets, their mouths grimacing in horror.

Another group surrounded Bill Russell who was speaking a blue streak, with all the self-importance of a character from a Gilbert and Sullivan operetta. Nick chuckled to himself because Russell, with his loose lips, had been cut out of the "loop" by Jonathan and could pontificate only about what everyone else now knew through the news media. But, unfortunately, that was a lot!

To avoid being bombarded with residents' questions Nick stood at the speaker's podium, pretending to be studying some notes. Many people in the audience were holding copies of the latest edition of the Morning Herald, with its banner headline, "Daughter Confirms Mother's Murder."

Rosemary Craig had supplied the paper with more details surrounding her mother's death, including the threatening note. All the cats were out of the bag except for Gillie's seeing the tall, thin, heavily shrouded person leaving Emma's townhouse on the morning of her death. Rosemary didn't know about that and, consequently, neither did the residents. It was good that this fact had not been revealed, Nick thought, or else the residents would be suspiciously eyeing all their fellow residents who could possibly be described as tall and thin. In a quick eyeballing of the crowd Nick realized that, thanks to good living, not too many residents could fit this description—maybe the tall part but definitely not the thin aspect.

Nick spotted Christina sitting in the third row, talking quietly to Helen Parker, his gym partner. The two women sat there like an oasis of calm, surrounded by seething clusters of agitated souls. Christina's presence was reassuring. Momentarily he made eye contact with her and she flashed him a smile and a thumbs-up gesture.

Five minutes before the planned starting time, it was standing room only and people were spilling out beyond the shade of the canvas top. The temperature was heading toward ninety and people were fanning themselves with their copies of the newspaper. Out of the corner of his eye Nick saw the Major approaching him and couldn't believe what he beheld: the Major was in full dress uniform as though this was Veterans Day and he was stepping up to receive the plaudits of the grateful citizenry. Over his shoulder the Major was carrying a large American flag on a six-foot stand.

"I thought we'd start the ceremony with the Pledge of Allegiance and the National Anthem," he said ponderously. The Major, with his **uber** militaristic approach to everything and his superficial patriotism, clearly intended to boost his self-image as a hero, which, because of his never having seen combat or even been in a war zone, always pushed Nick's buttons. This time was no exception.

Whatever ribbons and medals the Major wore on his uniform were not for seeing any action or acts of bravery. Nick thought that if, indeed, they were even real, they were for things like good typing skills, consistent punctuality and good housekeeping, for Nick had discovered that the Major had spent his entire career with his scrawny ass in offices of army bases in the United States.

In his two tours of duty as a helicopter pilot in Vietnam, Nick had been injured, had seen men die—some quickly, some quietly, and some after tremendous suffering—and had known the fatalism and despair that can grip men in mortal combat. And here was this strutting tin soldier masquerading as a true witness to the horrors of war, which Nick considered an abject insult to all the unsung, real heroes of combat.

Nick turned his full attention to the Major, fixing him with an icy glare. "Were you planning on leading the community in reciting the Pledge?" he asked quietly.

The Major's eyes sparkled. "I thought I would, yes."

Nick's voice became more intimate, more intense. "This isn't a Boy Scouts' Jamboree or a War Bond Drive and we're not starting the service with either the Pledge or the Anthem! Put the flag down and take a seat!"

Like a whipped puppy who just got smacked on the snout for peeing in a place where he shouldn't, the Major, always buckling under Nick's stern reproaches, morosely retreated.

A keyboard had been placed next to the podium and Nick greeted Francesca, the lesbian grandmother who had played piano with a regional orchestra before retiring. Now she volunteered to play for all community events. Her partner Alison stood by to turn the pages of the music.

Francesca and Alison were Nick's neighbors and two of the nicer, saner people at Marsden Grove. Their story, told to Nick over wine and cheese in their townhouse, was an interesting one. Both widows and grandmothers, they had attended a college reunion of their class and had known each other only casually while in college.

At this point in their lives, forty years later, they unexpectedly fell in love and had been a couple ever since.

Francesca settled into her chair before the keyboard and nodded to Nick who took a deep breath and looked out across the large audience.

"Good morning, ladies and gentlemen," Nick intoned, speaking directly into the microphone set up on the lectern.

The audience ignored him and he repeated his salutation in a louder, slightly exasperated voice. The hubbub gradually faded and all eyes were now fixed on him.

"We gather together this morning to remember and honor a much loved and respected member of our community, Emma Craig."

From the back row came the loud voice of Bill Russell. "Let's honor her by finding her murderer!"

Outbursts of acclamation swept across the audience as heads nodded vigorously and people waved their newspapers in Nick's direction. He had uttered only five words and repeated them once, and already a revolt was brewing.

Nick paused for only a moment to formulate his response to this sudden, unexpected diversion. Now, the intensity of his facial expression, his jaw muscles twitching ominously, and the unmistakable menace in his voice riveted his audience into silence.

"I repeat! We are here to remember our neighbor and friend. While the circumstances surrounding her death are unfortunate, we owe Emma Craig our deference by participating properly in this memorial service. This is our only chance as a community to show our respect. And this we must do!"

Nick fell silent and swept the audience with his glowing eyes, daring anyone to challenge him. He felt like a lion tamer in a cage with a pack of wild beasts, where only fearlessness and strength could subdue them. No one accepted his challenging stare and even Bill Russell seemed to have shriveled in his chair. He had quelled an incipient revolution in the first two minutes and now he continued.

"As always on these occasions, Reverend Tom Schneider will lead us in this ceremony."

Nick was happy to step away from the podium and let Reverend Pious take the reins. If the Major was super militaristic, the Reverend was super sanctimonious. Nick watched with amusement as the Reverend approached the podium with an aura of shimmering pomposity as if he were about to deliver the Sermon on the Mount.

Placing a sheath of papers on the lectern's shelf, he fumbled with adjusting the flexible microphone, saying, "Testing, one, two, three. Can everyone hear me?" The audience responded affirmatively, but Reverend Tom wanted to be sure that no one in the large audience missed one silver word emerging from his lips, so he repeated, "Can everyone hear me?"

From the short distance away where Nick had been standing, he said, "They can hear you in Cleveland."

The Reverend cast a quick sidelong glance of disapproval in Nick's direction, then fussed with his papers some more and finally bowed his head as though summoning divine inspiration. He remained in that posture far too long and only began to speak when the spell he was trying to sustain on his audience was clearly broken by the rising tide of murmurs and foot shuffling.

"We come together in a spirit of fellowship to remember a woman who graced our lives with her presence and who enhanced our community with her gentle, exemplary Christian ways."

Nick frowned, noting that Reverend Pious had now, in the course of one sentence, ruptured any "spirit of fellowship," by separating Emma Craig's good "Christian" ways from those of Jews, Muslims (there was a Muslim couple in the community and they were sitting in the audience), Buddhists, agnostics, atheists, pantheists and assorted idolaters.

Being a man of limited imagination and creativity, Reverend Pious always gave the same "shtick" for every memorial gathering. Somewhere he had found an essay or sermon titled "What is the Good Life?" combining elements of Ralph Waldo Emerson, Billy Graham and Jack Benny. Nick found the content interesting, but even the first time it was delivered, it was dead on arrival because the Reverend, always consciously trying to portray himself as a man of gravity, equated high seriousness with deep vocal intonations. Consequently, he delivered every line in a growling monotone where content was debased by delivery. The Reverend's melodramatic intonations always made Nick think of the angry, vengeful Jehovah of The Old Testament as rendered in the hoary Cecil B. DeMille biblical epics.

Reverend Pious droned on in this manner for fifteen unmerciful minutes. In order to adapt this canned speech to the current community member being memorialized, he would halt at the end of every paragraph and interject, "And these were the sterling qualities demonstrated by Emma Craig." No matter what virtues were being extolled in any paragraph, be they thrift, charity, modesty, temperance or even bravery in battle, they were all, according to the Reverend, part of Emma Craig's profile.

Nick recalled that this was the fourth or fifth time he had heard this speech since coming to Marsden Grove. Looking out at the assembly and seeing neighbors whose residency had been far longer than his, he could almost see them mouthing the words along with the speaker. The dazed look on many faces conveyed the heightened boredom rampaging across the audience.

Finally coming to an end with the refrain, "And these were the sterling qualities demonstrated by Emma Craig, " Reverend Pious now called for a minute of reflective silence to allow individual recollections of Emma's sterling qualities. Nick thought about the limited knowledge he had of Emma Craig: a nice lady who, although frail, was always smiling and enjoyed playing bridge with a group of neighbors. His image of Emma hardly corresponded to the lofty, all-encompassing qualities ennobled in the Reverend's speech on the Good Life. Mahatma Gandhi and Mother Theresa would have found it challenging to embrace all the enumerated virtues.

Nick's mind jumped to the threatening note Emma had received, and he was lost in speculation about something in her past that would warrant the taking of her life at her advanced age. His thoughts were interrupted by Francesca's playing some introductory notes on the keyboard.

The audience stood and began singing a hymn that the Reverend had said was one of Emma's favorites. Nick had never heard it before, and, from the off-note cacophony coming from the voices in the audience, neither had most other residents. The words, mercifully, had been printed and distributed but the music had not. People who thought they knew the tune clashed with others who were improvising and still others who were haphazardly chiming in on every fourth or fifth note. Nick likened the effect to nails scrapping across a blackboard, and the caterwauling seemed to go on forever, to everyone's discomfort.

Finally the hymn ended on an indeterminate note, the audience took their seats again and the Reverend, whose smug look radiated his own exalted estimate of his performance, gathered his papers and majestically left the podium. Nick quickly moved to replace him, nervously anticipating the next portion of the ceremony.

"It's been our custom at these memorial gatherings," Nick said, strenuously trying not to speak in the Reverend's pattern, "to ask individual members of our community to share their thoughts and memories about our departed neighbor. Does anyone have something they wish to share?"

Immediately Nick saw a dozen hands fly into the air as if a bingo game had just been won. Board member Jane Curtis, the Cat Lady, had volunteered to hand the portable microphone to each person who rose to speak. Surveying the raised hands, Nick searched for someone who might be positive and not a flame thrower. He spotted Alice Kramer, the Pack-Rat Lady, who lived next to Emma and, momentarily forgetting that it was she who had discovered Emma's body, thought she might have some nice and appropriate comments. He called on Alice who stood, as an expectant hush descended on the audience.

Jane Curtis hurried to Alice's side and handed her the microphone. Alice started to speak, but a chorus of voices hollered, "We can't hear you!" Jane had forgotten to turn the mike on. She pushed a button and Alice asked, "Now can you hear me?" A chorus responded "Yes." One resident, who was known to be almost completely deaf but kept forgetting to wear her hearing aids, shouted "Still can't hear you!" but was ignored.

With a wan smile Alice spoke in a tremulous voice, barely audible even with the magnification of the microphone, but no one, out of respect, asked her to speak louder.

"Emma was my next-door neighbor and we looked out for each other. Because she no longer drove and I still did, we'd go grocery shopping together and went to the Lutheran Church together on Sunday. She loved to play bridge, but I don't play, so sometimes in the evening we'd play gin rummy together. Emma was always smiling and cheerful, but I sensed a sadness underneath. I thought maybe she missed her late husband, Arthur, although she seldom spoke of him. She did talk fondly about the house they had built together in Omaha before he died and she moved to Marsden Grove to be closer to her only daughter. She came to this country sometime after the Second World War. I was intrigued by what she must have experienced in Germany during the war but she never wanted to talk about that part of her life and I didn't push it. She loved to read and do crossword puzzles. After her back operation last year she was in a lot of discomfort but she never complained. She just started exercising more to regain her strength."

Alice paused and took several deep breaths. Now her words came more slowly as though she were squeezing them out. "Emma was the nicest, sweetest lady I ever met, and why anyone would...would want...to take her life...I can't possibly imagine."

Tears cascaded down Alice's cheeks as she sank into her chair and her immediate neighbors rushed to comfort her with soft words and soothing gestures, gently patting her shoulders and rubbing her back.

Nick could sense a tidal wave of emotions, mostly fear and anger, sweeping across the restless audience and braced himself for what surely was to come next.

Dagmar Neilson didn't wait to be acknowledged and was on her feet, shouting, "What are the police doing about this?"

"They're doing everything they can," Nick shouted back.

Dagmar continued her assault. "A woman has been murdered in her home and that makes us all feel unsafe, especially since, with our twenty-four hour security, it would appear that the killer was one of us and could be sitting here right now."

This declaration caused everyone to eye those neighbors to the left and right of them with newly aroused suspicions. Nick thought it was good that Vincent Zabridini, the reclusive, wild-eyed, retired chemistry teacher, was absent from this gathering or else a lynch mob might be forming on the spot.

Following Dagmar's aggressive lead, other residents were now on their feet and, without being acknowledged by Nick as having the floor or accepting the use of the portable mike as the Cat Lady dashed madly about, were clamoring to be heard.

"What will this do to our home values?" wailed Vera Parks, who had been trying to sell her townhouse, unsuccessfully because of her inflated asking price.

"We could be murdered in our beds!" Henry Cushman shouted. Nick thought this very unlikely in Henry's case since he spent more time in Violet Tomby's bed than in his own.

Even Celeste Cushman, the replanted *"grande dame"* of the Hamptons, was on her feet, looking stunningly cool in another well-tailored ensemble, and saying something, but her soft, cultured tones were drowned out by more raucous voices.

Always one to rush in at any crisis and lead a charge, the Major was now bellowing above the din, "I say we start our own investigation,"

"Were you with Army Intelligence, Major?" Nick asked, quietly seething.

The Major gave a shrug in Nick's direction and addressed the audience. "No, but we've got to protect ourselves. Who wants to join me?"

"I will!" shouted Dagmar, as though she was ready to mount the barricades and start singing "One More Day" from *Les Miserables.*

"So will I!" shouted Jack Skelly, which surprised Nick since Jack's discarded porno files had been discovered by Dagmar, while rummaging through other people's trash for recyclables, and announced to the public at the recent Annual Homeowners Meeting.

A chorus of swelling voices now filled the air as Nick noted that growing hysteria was gripping the assembly.

From the back came the booming voice of Bill Russell. "I can offer all my expertise from thirty-two years with the New York City Police Department and I'll gladly lead the investigation."

Over the din Nick shouted back, "Were you a detective, Bill?"

"No, but I worked closely with detectives on many cases and I know how to lead an investigation."

Nick thought Bill's claims were probably based more on reading cheap detective novels and watching crime dramas on television than from actual investigative work, but, as he was formulating a response to Bill, the Major spoke up again.

"Given my many years of active military service, I think I should command the investigation."

Nick had an instant mental picture, knowing the Major's military career behind a desk, of his tenaciously ferreting out the culprits stealing pens and paper clips from the supply cabinet. A clear division of putative authority was now rupturing the community as one resident after another shouted, "Let the Major lead!"—mostly male veterans—or, "I'm with Bill!"—mostly ladies.

Emotions were reaching a frenzied pitch and Nick knew he had to stop it. But how? The Cat Lady, finally immobilized by all the shouting and people jumping up and waving their arms for her attention, stood frozen with shock and awe, the portable microphone tightly clutched against her chest. Nick recognized that he had the advantage of the mike on the lectern. He removed it from its mooring and, in one sweeping motion, shoved the heavy wooden lectern off the podium. It crashed to the ground amidst flying dirt and grass.

An instant silence pervaded the stunned throng and Nick bellowed, "Let's not get carried away, folks." He was about to say more when he suddenly spotted Jonathan Grimes who had magically appeared standing next to the Cat Lady, from whose frozen hands he had taken the portable mike.

In a thunderous voice reminding Nick of Charlton Heston as Moses in *The Ten Commandments,* Jonathan boomed, "My name is Detective Grimes and I've been assigned to investigate the death of Emma Craig. Let me assure you that we are following up on every possible lead, but let me also assure you that to launch your own investigation could possibly interfere with the official police inquiry and you could be charged with obstructing justice."

All the air seemed to have been sucked out of the assembled throng as Jonathan's threat of legal liability and prosecution effectively suppressed any revolutionary thoughts of acting independently.

In a more conciliatory tone, Jonathan continued. "I recognize that you want to get to the bottom of this and the police do, too. The best way you can help is to share with me any details about Emma Craig that come to mind and that you haven't already told me."

"What about if we suspect someone?" came a voice that Nick recognized as that of Jessie Knowles, his fellow Board member. Big Foot just had to grab some of the limelight in this developing high drama.

"Your suspicions would have to be grounded on factual evidence," Jonathan explained patiently.

"We've got some pretty strange characters in this place," Big Foot persisted. Nick whispered to himself, *"And you're at the top of that list!"*

Jonathan responded in an even tone. "That alone is not what I'd consider factual evidence. I've already spoken to a good number of you and I've said that because someone acts in a strange manner or is reclusive or you just don't like the person, that's not a reason for you to suspect that person of being a murderer. And despite the twenty-four-hour security here at Marsden Grove, we can't be sure that the murderer was from the community."

"Then you're confirming that this was a murder?" someone asked. "That what the daughter told the paper is true?"

"That's the way we're treating it," Jonathan said placidly. "So, remember, if you can think of any other details about Emma's life, her friends and any outside people she might have come in contact with, and you haven't shared this with me already, please give me a call at the station and I'll get back to you as soon as I can."

Nick noted that Jonathan, for good reason, was not giving out his cell phone number as he had to Nick. A good decision, Nick thought, because he'd have the wackos calling him day and night.

Jonathan's voice assumed a friendlier tone. "I'll tell you honestly that this is a baffling case and we need all the help we can get. But please work with us and not against us. With everyone's full cooperation we'll solve this case."

All the previous angry voices were silent. Nick sensed that Jonathan had struck the right chord with his final remarks, and the residents now felt proud to be helping the police.

"We'll give you our full cooperation," shouted Bill Russell, who clearly had switched positions and now wanted to be regarded as the detective's helpmate.

The Major, too, capitulated with a terse, "And we'll be very alert!"

Jane Curtis, Cat Lady, was now raising her hand timidly. Nick said "Yes, Jane?" Taking the microphone back from the detective, she spoke in a low, breathy voice. "I know that we came together today in memory of Emma and to honor her. And, my goodness, we've certainly gone off in another direction. So just let me say that

Emma was a wonderful bridge player and really loved the game and I always enjoyed playing with her."

After all the riotous emotions that had swept through the crowd, this sweet, simple statement from Jane seemed to be the perfect note on which to end this memorial. At a sign from Nick, Francesca played another stirring hymn as everyone disbursed. Nick immediately headed toward Christina who was still chatting with Helen Parker. Helen offered him a shy smile as Christina gave him a tight hug and several pats on the back.

"Great job!" was all she whispered to him. Nick smiled broadly as they disentangled themselves from their warm embrace and Christina added, "Helen was just telling me how brave Emma was. After her back operation she started using the gym equipment to give her greater mobility. Helen was helping her."

Nick had never seen Emma in the gym, but he remembered that he only went there very early in the morning and he knew that Helen's rigorous exercise regimen included two or three visits to the gym daily.

"That was good of you," he said to Helen.

"Do you think I should mention that to the detective?" Helen asked, clearly uncertain if this was the kind of information the detective wanted.

"Was she there with anyone else in the gym, except you?" Nick asked.

"Only Susan Moriarity, as far as I can remember," Helen said, "but Susan didn't interact with us except to say 'Hello.' She was intent on exercising on the Nautilus."

Nick thought of the battling Moriaritys and decided that Susan was probably building up her strength for the next knock-down, no-holds-barred battle with her husband.

"No," Nick said. "That doesn't seem to add up to factual evidence of any significance, but thanks for mentioning it."

Christina and Nick said goodbye to Helen and headed toward Jonathan who was listening with a clearly bored facial expression to an animated monologue by Bill Russell. Seeing Nick approaching, Jonathan brusquely said "Excuse me."

"Thanks for rescuing me," Nick said as Jonathan approached, "I didn't even know you were here."

"Now you've rescued me," Jonathan said with a slight nod in Bill Russell's direction.

Nick introduced Jonathan to Christina and could tell that Jonathan was giving her an approving appraisal.

"Give me a call on Monday," Jonathan said before departing.

"What's that about?" Christina asked as they walked back to Nick's townhouse.

"Mindful of his being sworn to secrecy, Nick answered casually, "If I hear anything from the residents, I pass it along."

"That's what he asked all the residents to do, isn't it?"

"Yeah, but because our Board president is missing and I'm the vice president, I might hear more," Nick said, trying to sound matter-of-fact. Hoping to change the subject, Nick quickly added, "Let's take Charley for a walk in the Preserve and then hit the links."

Christina readily agreed.

"And I'm cooking tonight," Nick announced decisively. "You'll get to try my famous meatloaf, one of my specialties," Nick said with a renewed sense of eagerness for the rest of this day with Christina.

Christina raised an eyebrow and smiled. "One of your specialties?" she teased.

"Yeah, one of my three specialties—the other two being spaghetti and meatballs and curried shrimp over rice."

"Can't wait to try them all," she said.

"Well, stick around and you will," he replied, giving her a challenging look, and she laughed.

He was suddenly conscious of a pervasive joyfulness in his relationship with Christina that he had never anticipated after losing his wife. Impulsively, he grabbed her hand and they walked quickly toward home where Charley would give them a wildly enthusiastic greeting. Despite all the unsettling events and community tumult, Nick was, for the moment, a happy man.

16

On Sunday morning Nick and Christina were in the kitchen making breakfast when the phone rang. It was Alice Kramer.

"Nick, I'm really sorry about breaking down like that at Emma's memorial and causing such a ruckus."

Nick was feeling magnanimous. "It's okay. I understand. Emma was your friend," he said cheerily while cradling the phone under his chin and flipping a pancake on the griddle.

"I don't know what to do about Carlos," Alice said.

"Carlos?" Nick had no idea who Carlos was.

"Yes, Carlos, Emma's parrot."

"Emma's parrot?" Nick repeated, still with no recognition.

"Yes. Emma had a parrot that someone had given her about six months ago. I don't know who."

"Who would be giving Emma a parrot?" Nick speculated aloud and then answered his own question. "Maybe her daughter Rosemary gave it to her for company, but this is the first I've heard of a parrot."

"No, it wasn't Rosemary," Alice said quickly. "I called her yesterday to ask her what to do with it, since I've been taking care of it since...since Emma's death. She told me to keep it or give it away and she didn't know who gave it to her mother either. Frankly, Nick, I don't want the bird. It reminds me of Emma and it talks a blue streak, but I don't know what to do with it. I feel sorry for the poor thing because I'm forced to keep its cage covered most of the time just to shut it up. Do you think I should post a note on the community bulletin board? It's a pretty bird and has a nice cage, and if someone didn't mind its constant talking, they could have it for nothing. And maybe after a while it would settle down."

"What does it say?" Nick asked, his curiosity aroused.

"I know it has an extensive vocabulary from hearing it when I would visit Emma, but right now it keeps saying, 'Hello, lady. Carlos scared!' over and over, and, I have to admit, it's getting on my nerves.

"How did Emma feel about the parrot?" Nick asked.

Alice was quick to respond. "That's funny you should ask, because I was never quite sure. She was mysterious about who gave it to her and she seemed to enjoy its company, but then sometimes the parrot would be talking away and she'd get upset and put the cover over its cage to keep it quiet."

Alice's story of the parrot was becoming more fascinating by the minute.

"Do you remember any of the words the parrot said that seemed to upset Emma?" Nick asked.

There was a long pause and Nick assumed that Alice was searching her memory. "Well," she finally said brightly, "the parrot seemed to know phrases from different prayers. The one I remember that always got a reaction from Emma was when he'd say "Forgive us our sins."

The word "sins" echoed in Nick's brain until he remembered Jonathan's telling him about the mysterious note Rosemary had discovered among her mother's things, saying something about paying for past sins. And what about the note found in the home of Emma's sister in Pennsylvania after she was killed in a hit-and-run? Wasn't that some threat about the past?

Nick concluded that all this was intriguing enough to share with Jonathan, but all he said to Alice was, "Put a note on the bulletin board, Alice, and let me know if anyone takes the parrot."

"Thank you, Nick. I will," Alice said with a note of relief, and the call ended.

"That sounded like a funny conversation from your end," Christina said as she poured orange juice.

"Yeah, Emma Craig had a parrot that now needs a home."

"And what was all that about its vocabulary?" Christina asked with mild curiosity.

Nick thought quickly before answering. "Oh, the parrot would use curse words that embarrassed Emma."

Placing the last pancake on the serving plate, he said, "I'm starved. Let's eat!"

17

The monthly meeting of the Marsden Grove Board of Managers was usually held in Fran Walker's home, but in her absence the hosting responsibility devolved to Nick.

Christina had helped Nick prepare cheese and crackers and chips with onion dip before retreating upstairs. By 7:15 PM on Sunday evening, the remaining four members of the Board were present, having all been extended a warm welcome by Charley, even Big Foot who disliked all animals and shied away from Charley's effusive sniffing. Nick called the meeting to order.

All the emotional frenzy expended at yesterday's memorial ceremony seemed to have sapped the energy of the Board members who, Nick noted, appeared unusually subdued. His hope that this state would persist throughout the meeting soon vanished. He had prepared an agenda, mostly dealing with reports from Board members on the sub-committees they chaired.

Nick gave full credit to Fran Walker for meeting the ego needs of the Major and Big Foot, as well as the demands and complaints of the more outspoken residents, by establishing the concept of Board sub-committees at Marsden Grove. These committees let many people feel that their voices were being heard, that they were making important contributions to improving life in the community.

Nick was intrigued by the different motivations that prompted residents to volunteer to serve on various sub-committees. Over time he had come to place them in three categories. There were those people who had a genuine interest in the entire community and were willing to give their time to broad areas of concern. Then there were those people who looked at everything through a narrow lens of self-interest and used a committee to advance a strictly personal agenda.

Finally there were those folks who used committee meetings to support their own ego needs by constantly displaying what they considered to be their superior intellects and penetrating insights in always asking "gotcha" questions. These inflated egos joined as many committees as they could schedule, from a sense of duty that without their outstanding contributions, the community would flounder.

Nick admired the first group, tolerated the second group and despised the third group—the Peacock Brigade as he called them—for they always conveyed an assured and condescending air of delight in dazzling their fellow residents with their brilliance. If they ever took note of the other residents' quiet groans and deep grimaces when the peacocks raised their hands to speak, they would have perceived another reality. However, sub-committees were ideal for letting the peacocks strut and preen and eventually exhaust themselves.

Nick was also aware of a fourth group as being perhaps the most subtle and pernicious. These were the residents who never volunteered for any sub-committee and always sat silently though all community meetings, never offering an opinion publicly. But then, in small private conversations, they criticized, with large doses of vitriol, all the actions taken by the people volunteering to serve as the community's leaders. Consistently negative, petty and captious, they served as a Greek chorus spreading gloom and doom wherever they gathered and with whomever they spoke.

Each time some issue arose across the community and persisted, Fran would establish a sub-committee, with a Board member as chair. Jane Curtis, the Cat Lady, was reluctant to chair any sub-committee except for the one overseeing the rules for animals at Marsden Grove.

The Major and Big Foot, however, could never get too many sub-committees. They were happy to sit for hours at these meetings, listening to the committee members' wrangling among themselves and intermittently taking center stage to pontificate on some aspect of the issue under discussion. Progress of any significance was seldom achieved, but everyone seemed happy to have a querulous voice at the table.

No sooner had the Board members assembled around Nick's dining table when Big Foot pulled the platter of cheese and crackers directly in front of him and proceeded to consume them like some starving man rescued at sea after months adrift in a raft. Nick made a mental note for future Board meetings that there should be two platters of goodies, one for Big Foot and one for the rest of the Board. Then he had a crazy flashback to his childhood and his mother's admonishing him when there was any meal that he especially liked, "Don't shovel the food into your mouth!"

His mother would be astonished at the rapidity with which Big Foot, bending over the platter to within an inch of the morsels, sucked them into his maw like some commercial vacuum cleaner. Within minutes the platter was empty and Big Foot was eyeing the chips and dip at the other end of the table but, Nick thought, was too embarrassed to say "Pass them down!" The other members of the Board always witnessed this gormandizing performance at the start of every meeting with a mixture of awe and disbelief. From the expression on the Cat Lady's face, there was an admixture of repugnance, too.

After this sideshow was completed, the members got down to business. The first agenda item called for Cat Lady to report on her one sub-committee regarding animals. Jane consulted some notes before speaking in her soft, self-effacing voice.

"As you know, we recently installed pooper-scooper bag dispensers around the community and…."

The Major loudly interrupted her with, "I stepped in a big pile of dog shit yesterday, so some dog owners obviously aren't using the bags."

Jane continued, unperturbed. "I sent out a notice to all residents, asking them to cooperate, but we have to give them time to adjust."

"And if they don't adjust, we should start fining them!" Big Foot said with vehemence, punctuated with a loud belch.

Nick couldn't resist saying, "How would we identify the dog with the poop? DNA?"

Ever eager to expand his authority, the Major said, "I could get a group together to watch when the dogs are being walked."

"Oh, I see," Nick said. "A spy system: neighbor tattling on neighbor. That ought to generate good community spirit!"

Big Foot joined the chorus. "That damn Great Dane of George Trumble's makes such a huge pile, you'd know it immediately." After a short pause, Big Foot snorted, "That pervert!"

Nick couldn't be sure if Big Foot's derogatory comment reflected his distaste for the Great Dane, his suspicion of something unnaturally occurring between the Great Dane and his owner, or his acceptance of the general community opinion that because George lived alone and had never been seen with a woman but received frequent packages from Victoria's Secret, he must be getting his kicks from cross-dressing.

Given George Trumble's burly, hirsute appearance, Nick could never picture him in frilly lingerie or a revealing Teddy. Maybe he had some lady on the side to whom he gave these gifts. Nick thought of all the enticing intimate garments that Christina wore to keep his interest peaked. *Why not give the guy the benefit of the doubt*, he thought, *before jumping to scurrilous conclusions.*

Jane remained softly resolute. "Let's give everyone a decent period of adjustment. I'm sure residents will comply."

"Yeah," Big Foot said with undisguised sarcasm. "Like the way they complied with our ban on propane gas grills on our balconies when the fire department said they were a hazard."

In citing this instance of non-compliance, Nick found himself agreeing with Big Foot. A good number of residents felt it was a basic right of every American to engage in that great summer pastime of grilling steaks, chicken, hamburgers, sausages and hot dogs on an open fire, the cooking method employed by their far-distant ancestors in the caves of Europe, the sands of Africa and the plains of Asia.

Most of the townhouses at Marsden Grove had a walk-out lower level with a small rear terrace where grilling was permissible. But because the kitchen, dining area and family room were conflated into one great room on the main level, residents insisted on the convenience of grilling on the small balcony on that floor. The result of this practice was two small fires and a warning from the fire department not to cook *al fresco* on the balconies.

"I've taken care of that!" the Major announced proudly and was greeted with a uniform chorus of "How?"

Smiling enigmatically, he said, "Just wait and see."

In a firm voice Nick said, "This is a community issue and as members of the Board of Managers we are required to act as a Board, in concert, and not as individuals. No Board member should be acting alone." Nick lowered his voice but raised his intensity. "Now tell us what you have done!"

The Major always wilted under Nick's challenges and this time was no different. Displaying both resentment and sheepishness, he admitted, "I contacted the fire chief and he's going to make a surprise visit on the Labor Day weekend and give citations to any residents caught grilling on their balconies."

Nick was astonished that, for once, he agreed with the Major's action; still, he had to enjoin him from acting independently. "That's not a bad idea, but you should have shared it with the Board first and gotten our approval."

The Major looked glum as Nick completed the formalities. "I'll consider this as a motion from the floor, which I'll second. All in favor?"

Big Foot, who could no longer resist the lure of the chips and dip at the other end of the table, had quietly asked the Cat Lady to pass them. Between shoving massive amounts in his mouth, he managed to burp, "Aye," while Jane and Nick merely raised their hands. "The motion is carried unanimously.

As the Board secretary, Jane dutifully took notes.

"Any other comments about the animal sub-committee?" Nick asked and Jane quickly said "No." Looking down at the agenda, Nick said, "Then let's move on to the report from the sub-committee on the pool. Jessie you have the floor."

Big Foot made a quick swallow and gave a broad swipe of his mouth with the back of his hand, still leaving remnants of the onion dip on his upper lip and chunky cheeks, giving him an appearance reminding Nick of a newly excavated Abominable Snow Man.

"We have an interesting situation developing," Big Foot announced with obvious glee, grabbing the Board's full attention. "The community is considering having a time period designated for nude swimming."

"What the hell!" the Major exclaimed, erupting from his chair in righteous indignation. Nick noted that part of the Major's ultra-conservative principles encompassed a remarkable prudery with all matters pertaining to anything remotely related to sex. Nick guessed that revealing any private parts of the human anatomy to others in any public forum was anathema as far as the Major was concerned, notwithstanding the panoptic display of patriotic tattoos the Major proudly displayed at the community pool.

Could it be, Nick mused, that the Major's robust modesty was possibly due to physical inadequacy? The Major was only five-feet-five inches tall, with small hands and feet. Perhaps his feeling of physical shortcomings was the root cause of his resolute stance on modesty.

"It's only a small group of residents who are making this request," Big Foot said, clearly bemused. "They're led by Henry Cushman."

Nick couldn't help but smile at the mention of Henry Cushman since it was widely known in the community that Henry was sleeping with Violet Tomby. Not satisfied with this conquest, Henry was a recognized lecher who had made passes at half the female residents, even the oldest and the feeblest. Nick's next amusing thought was that perhaps Henry was the physical opposite of the Major and was looking for a venue to advertise his assets.

"This is not Sodom and Gomorrah!" the Major thundered in high dudgeon, while Cat Lady flushed an intense crimson.

Big Foot laughed. "They're willing to have a designated time in the very early morning or late at night," he said.

"I'll bet they are!" the Major said sarcastically, still in full throttle. "Are you supporting this insane idea?" he challenged, pointing at Big Foot.

Nick almost burst out laughing at the flashing vision of Big Foot in the "all-together," with his many excess layers and drooping parts flopping around in the water. Why would any senior citizen, knowing the toll that time takes on realigning and corrugating the human form, want to display those weathered, dislocated silhouettes? Nick could think of possibly two exceptions: Dagmar Neilson had a great figure for a septuagenarian, at least in clothes, and Helen Parker, his gym partner, had the body of a young athlete. But Nick couldn't easily conjure a fantasy of any female resident whom he would enjoy seeing *"au natural"* in a pool setting. Even his intoxicating Christina had a few extra pounds that she was self-conscious about.

"This wouldn't be good for our community's image," Cat Lady said meekly.

"Or maybe it might be," countered Big Foot, relishing the consternation this topic was causing.

Nick suddenly pictured a new advertising campaign: Come to Marsden Grove and Hang Out! Bring the Grandkids and Let Them See the Future!

"This is against everything that's decent!" the Major sputtered, flailing his arms and spewing spittle on his chin. Nick sensed that the Major was winding up to deliver a lengthy harangue on God, Nature and the American Way, so he cut him off mid-sentence. "There's no point in discussing this any further," he said in a commanding voice, silencing the Major's fulminations. "Jessie, please tell the sub-committee that the Board reviewed this topic and declines to take any action."

"Are we going to vote on it as a motion?" Cat Lady asked, ever mindful of Robert's Rules of Order and her scrupulously scripted Board Minutes.

"Yes, and condemn it for the record!" the Major yelled contemptuously.

"Jessie, did the sub-committee formally take a vote and approve submitting this action to the Board?" Nick asked, suspecting that the sub-committee had not, and that Jessie was raising this topic for his own titillating pleasure.

'No," Big Foot admitted, chuckling.

"Then we'll treat it informally, too." Nick decreed.

"I want to go on record as condemning this idea in the strongest possible terms," the Major blustered. Nick, now tired of the Major's posturing, responded. "Then go to the next pool sub-committee meeting and fully express your feelings. This topic will not be part of our record so let's move on, unless Big....(Nick caught himself just in time), unless Jessie has any legitimately raised topic from his committee to bring to us now."

Jessie, still smiling and obviously pleased with the fleeting mayhem he had caused, said "No."

Undaunted, the Major switched topics. "I want to discuss what we're doing about the murder."

In a deadly menacing tone and staring intensely at the Major through half-closed eyes, giving the best Humphrey Bogart imitation he could muster, Nick spoke. "You and everyone else have had your say about the murder and it's now in the hands of the police and that's the end of it for now!"

A pregnant silence followed Nick's declaration as the Major, with downcast eyes, once again bowed to Nick's intimidating tone and mutely decided not to pursue the topic further.

Sensing his victory, Nick said in a lighter tone, "Let's get on with our agenda."

Both Big Foot and Cat Lady seemed to breathe audible sighs of relief and the meeting proceeded at a quickened pace, in an orderly manner. Any further attempt by any Board member to stray from the agenda was summarily cut off at the pass by the vigilant, weary Nick.

18

In the last few minutes of the Board meeting Nick could barely contain his impatience. He wanted the meeting to end. He wanted a beer. He wanted to clear his head and take Charley for a walk. He wanted the company of Christina, who had sequestered herself upstairs while the Board meeting was going on. He wanted to be away from his posturing, pontificating fellow Board members. He wanted to break Fran Walker's neck for running out on him for spurious reasons, he was certain, and leaving him to deal with the mess. He wanted his peaceful life back.

With no ceremony after the agenda was finished, he hustled the Board members out the door and whistled for Charley who came bounding down the stairs, his tail oscillating like a whirligig, followed by a smiling Christina.

Happy at the very sight of her, Nick said, "I need a long walk to get my brain in order. Want to come?"

"Sure," she responded eagerly.

Charley, somehow, knew that a walk was planned—Nick swore that Charley understood at least fifty English words including "walk'—and the dog bounded for the front door where he turned and waited expectantly. Nick leashed him and soon the ecstatic Charley and the happy couple, arm in arm, flashlight in hand, were headed for the Preserve and a quiet, cloudless, star-packed stroll.

Charley, freed from his leash once they had reached the Preserve, skittered and rollicked in all directions, his nose keenly giving him feedback on the scents of many nocturnal animals in the vicinity, but he took no interest in them, just relishing his freedom and always keeping Nick and Christina within visual range. Periodically he would come bounding back to them and dash around them in circles while they laughed at his exuberant antics and joined in his spirit of fun with encouraging words and clapping hands. Charley's sheer joy was infectious, and all three walkers returned home in high spirits.

Charley rushed to his water bowl and drank copiously, then waited for Nick to give him his treat, a dog biscuit, a ritual after every major walk of the day. He watched Nick and Christina ascend the stairs to the master bedroom and followed them dutifully, only to be disappointed when Nick closed the door of the bedroom, leaving Charley on the other side.

Charley had always slept on the floor next to Nick and Judy's bed. One night, shortly after Judy died, Charley, unsolicited, made a bold move and jumped on the king-size bed, settling himself at the far bottom corner away from Nick. Nick had sat up and stared at Charley in the darkness, as the dog's tail thumped pleadingly against the bed covers. In the ensuing silence Charley sensed that Nick was weighing this audacious move and deciding either to accept or reject Charley's new overture. Finally, Nick said "Okay, fella," and lay back down.

When Nick's steady, deep breathing convinced Charley that his master was sleeping, Charley carefully crawled across the bed on his belly and settled himself happily against Nick's legs. In the tossing and turning of both man and dog during the night, Nick awoke the next morning to find his arm encircling Charley's stretched-out body. As soon as Nick stirred, Charley rolled over and planted a good-morning kiss on Nick's cheek. From that day on, the dog and man were comforting bedmates. Until Christina arrived.

The first night that Christina spent at Nick's home was a mystifying one for Charley. First of all, he was ordered by Nick to assume his previous post on the floor by the bottom of the bed. As disappointing as that was, the sounds and actions of the couple on the bed were like nothing Charley had ever witnessed, and the dog was thoroughly confused.

Being loyal to his master and having taken an instant shine to this new lady, Charley couldn't tell from the tumbling and gyrating and all the groans and exclamations if they were having fun or hurting each other. In his confused state of mind, he did the only thing he knew to do to express his sad uncertainty: whimper. When his plaintive pleadings got no attention, he proceeded to a more forceful stand: growling. Continuing to be ignored, he finally resorted to loud barking.

At this point a naked Nick jumped off the bed and, clearly in an exasperated state, grabbed Charley by his collar and ignominiously escorted him to the door. A chagrined Charley lay outside the closed door, assessing this new situation before concluding that whatever they were doing in the bedroom to each other, he was no longer welcomed, needed or wanted. His gentle, adaptable nature, his fierce love for Nick and his fondness for this new lady eventually soothed his indignant feelings.

From that night on, whenever Nick and Christina entered the bedroom, Charley knew and accepted the routine. Nick would give Charley a pat on the head while Christina uttered a dulcet "Good night, Charley," and the door would then close. Charley would assume his sentry duty in the hall, content in feeling that they were not harming each other, no matter how bizarre their actions became. Charley decided that people could be really weird and let it go at that.

19

Nick called Jonathan early Monday morning and heard the brusque "Yeah," at the other end, followed by a milder "Hold on a minute," and "Don't forget your lunch. Do you have your flute?"

Nick's curiosity was aroused by this overheard monologue, for her realized that he knew nothing about Jonathan's personal life.

"Sorry about that," Jonathan said, returning to the phone, and Nick couldn't help himself. "Who plays the flute?" he asked in a light, jocular voice.

"My granddaughter, Samantha. Her parents are on a cruise and I'm taking care of her and her brother."

"How old are they?"

"Samantha's twelve and Eric is eight." Jonathan then terminated Nick's line of personal questions with, "Anything new on your front?"

"Yes," Nick replied, shifting gears. "Did you know that Emma Craig had a parrot?"

"No. There wasn't any parrot there when the police arrived."

"I think Alice Kramer must have taken the bird right after she discovered Emma's body because it was very upset and kept screaming."

"What was it screaming?" Jonathan asked, and Nick thought for a moment before answering, "'Carlos scared!' Carlos is the parrot's name."

"Anything else?"

"He just kept repeating 'Hello Lady,' which I took to be a general greeting," Nick offered.

"Could be," Jonathan said evenly. "Is the parrot still with Alice Kramer?"

"Yes, but she wants to get rid of it. It never shuts up unless you put the cover on its cage. Just keeps repeating 'Hello, lady. Carlos scared' in a loud screech."

Jonathan changed the subject. "The coroner's report finally came back. Emma was strangled before she was strung up. Her windpipe was crushed in two different places, once by the rope and once by other means, most probably human hands."

Nick was caught completely off-guard by this new information—the conclusive evidence that

Emma Craig had been murdered. "Any other clues?" he asked.

"No. The murderer used gloves and must have taken Emma by surprise as she was sleeping. There was no struggle."

"So she was murdered in her bed and then dragged to the living room and strung up, to make it look like a suicide?"

"That's about it," Jonathan said, "except she must have been carried and not dragged, based on our analysis of the carpet between the bedroom and living room. She only weighed about a hundred pounds."

"But if there was no sign of forced entry, the murderer must have had a key to Emma's home," Nick continued, thinking aloud.

"Right!" Jonathan said. "I don't think Emma would have kept her door unlocked after receiving that threatening note about past sins. The police found all her windows locked and the lock on her door had not been tampered with." Jonathan suddenly switched topics. "Jesus! Have you ever been in Alice Kramer's home?"

"No, but I've heard about it through the community grapevine."

"It's a mess!" Jonathan said. "I've never seen so much clutter everywhere. You can hardly move from one room to another without bumping into something. Things are stacked to the ceiling in many places. By the way, when I visited her I didn't see any parrot. It could have been upstairs but if she said it was screaming constantly, I would have heard it."

"She told me she had to keep the cover on its cage most of the time because its screeching was driving her crazy," Nick explained, before adding, "I guess we're still clueless."

"The check on Emma's background revealed a couple of interesting facts," Jonathan said. "Her mother died of cancer shortly after the family migrated to America in the late forties, and her father committed suicide about a year after by jumping off a bridge. Emma married a few months after her father's suicide and she and her husband moved to Omaha. And here's another fact: Emma's sister changed her last name around the time Emma got married. The family name had been Mueller but the father changed it to Strelitz, when they came to the States and then she changed it again, this time to Steele."

"Lots of people change their names," Nick offered, thinking aloud. "I believe some forebear of mine dropped a few letters from my last name. Everybody wants to sound more American."

"Yeah," Jonathan responded in a noncommittal tone.

"Did the sister ever marry?" Nick asked.

"No."

"So, except for the daughter, there are no other current suspects," Nick said, still thinking aloud. "And she's out because of Gillie's description of some tall, thin person he saw leaving Emma's townhouse on the morning of her murder. The daughter is short and heavy."

Jonathan corrected Nick. "That makes **everybody** else a current suspect who could possibly fit the description of tall and thin."

A new thought skittered across Nick's mind and he immediately shared it. "Suppose there was cause to discount Gillie's eye-witness account. We know Gillie has a drinking problem. He's been caught a number of times drinking on the job. We always felt so sorry for him, what with his wife leaving him and taking his only child back to Romania, that we were always giving him another chance. Besides, he was a damn good worker and could fix anything—a true Jack-of-all-trades. But maybe he was hung over from the night before when he came to work on the morning of Emma's death, or maybe he was still drinking. Maybe he had a distorted vision of the person leaving Emma's home."

Jonathan interrupted Nick's ramblings. "Or maybe he didn't see anyone at all."

Nick paused. "I didn't think of that," he admitted. "But wouldn't that suggest that he had an ulterior reason for claiming that he did? Was it just some drunken delusion?"

"Yes to the first question; could be to the second," Jonathan said. "He might have an ulterior motive for his claim, and he could have been having a drunken hallucination. That still doesn't explain how the murderer gained access to Emma's townhouse and attacked her in her bed. I'm meeting with Gillie today in my office."

Nick's concern for Gillie was instantly aroused. "Jonathan, he also could have been cold sober and is telling the truth, so please don't be too rough on him. It wouldn't take much, I fear, to make the guy completely fall apart."

There was an audible chuckle at the other end. "You've been watching too many TV crime shows, Nick. We don't give the 'third degree' as they used to call it. We employ psychology nowadays."

Feeling foolish, Nick quickly said "I know, I know," and added his own chuckle to the conversation.

Jonathan changed the subject. "By the way, who is Sonia Arcadivich?"

Nick continued chuckling in supplying an answer. "A real nut job! Why?"

She keeps calling the station and warning of dire things to come at Marsden Grove. She's offered her psychic services in finding Emma's killer, for a fee."

"Yeah, she claims she can see the future by reading the pattern of anything: tea leaves, match sticks, probably the buttons on your coat or the noodles in your soup. She's all gloom and doom. You'd be better off consulting a Ouija Board."

Nick was about to offer more evidence of Sonia's bizarre personality and how she'd been able to convince so many residents of her special powers, but he was interrupted by Jonathan.

"Well, she's not the only strange fruit in your orchard of kooks. We're constantly getting calls from your residents claiming they know who the killer is. When I follow up with them, they give the wildest reasons. One guy is convinced it's his neighbor that he's been feuding with over the neighbor's dog pooping on this guy's terrace."

"That's been going on for a long time," Nick explained. "Those two have come to blows a couple of times. And endless threats of law suits."

Jonathan continued. "And who's Vincent Zabridini? Half the community is convinced he's a maniac and if not a murderer, a terrorist."

Nick's laugh was loud. "He's an eccentric recluse who was a chemistry teacher before retiring. He looks like a cross between Dr. Frankenstein and Dr. Strangelove, but I'd say he's harmless"

Jonathan's voice now had an exasperated edge. "Every night the station gets calls from folks at Marsden Grove, claiming that someone's prowling outside their windows or trying to break in."

"I know," Nick said. "Some call the police and others call the security guard, and he's running around all night with a flashlight searching the shrubbery outside of homes and checking windows and doors, but he's never spotted anyone, except once there was a raccoon. Then there was Henry Cushman who was discovered trying to sneak away from Violet Tomby's townhouse at 4 AM, but that's an innocent shack-up."

Nick felt compelled to add a cautionary note. "You can't blame them, Jonathan. This is a very challenging time for us seniors. A lot of the residents feel vulnerable about any further attacks. Not knowing who the murderer is, or why he killed Emma, leaves them open to their worst fears that they're all going to be murdered in their beds. Incidentally, I wouldn't feed that fear by mentioning that Emma **was** murdered in her bed. You'd send half the hearts in the community into cardiac arrest.

"Your fellow Board member, John Stevens, the one you call the Major, is the worst of all," Jonathan said.

"What's he done now?" Nick asked, not bothering to conceal his annoyance.

The security guard found him the other night around 8 PM in the main parking lot drilling a group of five or six men in a military formation and barking orders 'to the left and the right' and 'about face' until one man passed out and another had an asthmatic attack and the EMTs had to be called. Your Major said he was preparing them to serve as a volunteer auxiliary security force. Fortunately, after this one practice drill, all the volunteers abandoned the idea and went home to check their pacemakers, but not the Major. He said he'd look for other recruits."

"I'll take care of him," Nick promised with angry authority.

"Good! I hope none of the residents have guns, including the Major."

Nick laughed. "If they do, they're relics from the Second World War or Korea, but I'll reinforce the prohibition against residents' taking any action unless specifically asked by the police, which, I know, isn't likely."

Nick suddenly realized how much more difficult the crazy residents of Marsden Grove were making Jonathan's job. "I'll do my best to keep them in check," he promised. "Let me know how your meeting with Gillie goes," he added.

"Thanks, I will," said Jonathan and, in his casual, abrupt style, was gone.

The hysteria that was gripping Marsden Grove placed a huge weight on Nick's shoulders, but working with Jonathan somehow relieved a lot of the pressure. Yet that pressure, he was sure, would only continue to grow until the murder of Emma Craig was solved. The puzzle remained completely scrambled.

20

Nick had taken Charley for his morning bathroom break before calling Jonathan and had dressed in his gym shorts and tank top so that he could head out for his daily gym workout after speaking to the detective. It was another blazing August morning portending withering temperatures by Noon, with the humidity adding to the discomfit. Nick jogged at a slow pace toward the gym in the pool pavilion, but because it was so hot, he took a shortcut through the main recreation room that had a rear door into the gym, rather than jog around to the outside gym entrance.

As he entered the darkened recreation room and was adjusting his eyes, he heard, "Hello fella." Once his vision became accustomed to the dim light, he spotted a parrot in a large cage over in one corner of the room. Walking toward it, the parrot kept repeating, "Hello fella," and Nick assumed that this was Carlos. As he drew closer he saw the hand-lettered sign attached to the cage, announcing that the parrot and cage were available for adoption at no charge.

Carlos had been climbing the metal side of his cage but stopped when Nick drew close and eyed his visitor.

"Hello Carlos," Nick said, and the parrot cocked his head.

"Hello fella," Carlos repeated, moving now to a feeder and selecting a nut with his curved beak but always keeping a wary eye on Nick.

He doesn't seem very riled up, Nick thought. *He must have calmed down a lot.*

"Goodbye Carlos," Nick said as he headed for the gym entrance.

"Goodbye fella," Carlos dutifully responded as Nick chuckled.

He entered the gym and was surprised to find no one there. Instantly he missed Helen Parker and her quiet, pleasant companionship and earnest focus on keeping herself in topnotch shape. On days when he might be flagging in energy or dedication, he could always count on Helen to quietly urge him onward and bolster his resolve. Helen varied her exercise regimen to avoid monotony, so Nick assumed she was probably on one of her fifteen-minute jogs, preferring to run outside, weather permitting, rather than running on the treadmill.

Susan Moriarity, of the battling Moriaritys, was also appreciated as a gym companion for her wry sense of humor and her acid-tongued remarks about her husband after one of their titanic battles. Nick often wondered what kept them together but chalked it up to the vagaries of the human heart. Jack Moriarity was enjoyable company in the weekly poker games with Nick. Two nice people, apart, who were incendiary together, but maybe it was all the friction and drama that was the glue holding their marriage together. He knew that he could never participate in such a volatile relationship and was grateful for the peaceful life he had enjoyed with Judy and now was enjoying with Christina.

A few minutes after starting his routine, his wandering thoughts were interrupted by ear-piercing screeching coming from the recreation room. Nick leaped off the treadmill without stopping it and rushed toward the direction of the continuous screeching. As he entered the recreation room he heard, "Carlos scared! Carlos scared!" followed by louder screeching.

The bird was clinging to the back of his cage, his head feathers up, his wings flapping furiously as if he were trying to escape from his confinement.

My god, he's seen the person who killed Emma, Nick thought instantly. Looking about the room he saw no one. He rushed outside to the pool area, quickly taking in the pool and surrounding grounds. No one.

Carlos was still screeching frantically, and Nick was about to return inside and try to soothe the frightened bird. Just then he noticed that the door marked Ladies Room, which had a separate entrance directly from the pool area, was closed. When it wasn't occupied, it was open. He walked over and knocked.

"I'll be out in a minute," he heard the calm voice of Susan Moriarity say.

Nick's breath was shallow and beads of perspiration were popping out on his forehead as he waited for the door to open. Susan emerged with a tentative smile. "Is the men's room occupied and this is an emergency?" she asked in a clearly humorous tone.

Nick ignored her question and launched into his own. "Did you see anybody in this area or someone coming out of the pool house before you went into the ladies room?"

"Only Carlton Wright coming out of the pool. You know how he likes to do laps in the morning."

"And nobody else?"

Susan caught the urgency in Nick's voice and looked perplexed. "No. Why?"

Nick suddenly had another thought: If you were exiting quickly from the recreation room, the nearest place to hide was in the ladies room.

"Would you mind stepping into the recreation room for a minute?" Nick asked directly.

Susan blanched. "Why?"

"I want to show you something," he ad-libbed,

Susan's face turned a pale shade of pearl. "No, I can't right now," she said, taking a few steps backward.

Nick advanced on her. "Why not, Susan?"

Momentarily she looked confused, as though she were deliberating on an answer, but then she smiled slightly. "Because, Nick, if you must know, I woke up this morning with some stomach bug and I've been running to the john ever since. I can't even do my morning exercises. Now I've got to get home pronto!"

She started to turn away but Nick grabbed her arm. "If you're in a hurry to get home, the quickest route to your place is through the recreation room and out the gym entrance."

A conflicted look swept across her face as Nick held on to her arm. Then she said, "Yes, I suppose you're right," and walked with him into the recreation room.

Nick's body was rigid with tension as he waited to see what Carlos would do upon seeing Susan, but as they walked quickly across the center of the large room, not a sound came from the corner where Carlos's cage had been placed. No greeting. No screeching. Nothing.

Nick escorted Susan to the interior door leading to the gym.

"My husband is probably trying to poison me, the bastard!" Susan said in half jest before disappearing into the gym. Nick rushed over to the cage. No Carlos.

The door of the cage was open. Nick looked on the floor. Over in the corner, behind the cage, he spotted Carlos's lifeless body. He picked the bird up and from the way the bird's head drooped, he could see instantly that its neck had been broken.

Involuntary shivers coursed through Nick's body as his mind acknowledged how close he had come to Emma Craig's killer.

21

Nick abandoned his gym routine and returned home where, unusual for him, he brewed himself a third cup of coffee and sat in the recliner in the family room, reviewing what he had just experienced.

The killer had obviously entered the recreation room and, upon seeing that person again, the parrot had gone ballistic. The killer now knew that the bird's frantic response could lead to suspicion. The killer rushed out and while Nick was frantically searching the outside area and then questioning Susan Moriarity and pressing her to return inside with him, the killer had circled around the building, saw that the gym was empty, gained access to the other side of the recreation room and strangled the bird.

Nick now realized that Carlos continued screeching while Nick was outside, but by the time he and Susan approached the outside door to the recreation room, there was no noise. Everything had taken place in a matter of minutes and the killer had had incredible luck that no one was in the pool area except Susan, locked in the ladies room, and no one was in the gym. After finding the dead bird's body, Nick had raced back to the gym and out through the outside gym entrance, but not a soul was visible.

As he was spanning the landscape for anyone who might have seen anything, Nick had spotted a white handkerchief dangling from the side of a low shrub lining the path to the gym. Seizing on anything as a possible clue, he went and got a plastic bag from the kitchenette in the recreation room and carefully dropped the linen handkerchief into the bag. Maybe the killer had used the handkerchief to open the door of the cage without leaving fingerprints and had then discarded it.

Nick put the bag in his pocket and then saw Helen jogging toward the gym from the direction of the Preserve. Helen's jogging speed amazed Nick and the few times that he had tried to jog with her, he knew that she was intentionally slowing her pace to make him feel comfortable. She arrived by his side, her breathing elevated only slightly. He had asked her if she had seen anyone during her jog coming in the opposite direction, away from the pool pavilion, but she had only seen Gillie heading for a townhouse by the Preserve and Carlton Wright walking quickly to his home.

Despite Nick's momentary suspicion of Susan Moriarity, she had been with him while Carlos was still shrieking wildly, so she couldn't have killed the bird. Then he turned his focus on Carlton Wright, who Susan had said was the only person seen in the pool when she arrived. Suppose, after Susan entered the ladies room, Carlton, for whatever reason, had entered the recreation room, causing Carlos to screech so wildly. He could have run around the building to the gym entrance while Nick was questioning Susan, and, seeing no one there but hearing Carlos still screeching, re-entered the recreation room through the gym without anyone seeing him. But what motivation could Carlton, a respected psychologist if a bit of a windbag, have for killing Emma Craig?

Then Nick corrected himself. Why would **anyone** have any reason for killing Emma? That was the key question, and until an answer could be found, her murder could not be solved.

Nick's thoughts were interrupted by glancing down and seeing Charley standing by Nick's chair with his leash dangling from the dog's mouth and his tail wagging fiercely. Nick looked at his watch and saw that it was time for Charley's second—and long—walk of the morning. Charley was punctilious about keeping to his schedule, and, whenever possible, trying to keep Nick on schedule, too.

"Okay, Charley, we'll go," Nick said, attaching the leash to the dog's collar. Charley was now bounding towards the door, and Nick hoped a brisk walk would clear his head of all these confusing and ominous thoughts. He resolved to lay everything in Jonathan's lap as soon as he returned from the morning exercise with the ever-eager Charley.

Nothing was more joyful to dog or man than their morning romps in the adjacent Preserve. As soon as he was released from his leash, Charley was in endless motion, racing in every direction, chasing after squirrels, chipmunks and an occasional rabbit. He never caught any creature, but that didn't matter since it was the thrill of the chase that buoyed his spirits. After each robust but fruitless pursuit, he'd scamper back to check on his mater before darting off in another direction and a new adventure.

Try as he might, Nick couldn't dispel all the troubling issues surrounding Emma Craig's murder, and the killing of the parrot brought the murder closer to him. He couldn't help but speculate what might have happened if he had come upon the murderer in the act of destroying Carlos and what might have ensued. Repeatedly, his thoughts turned to replaying each moment of this morning's events at the pool pavilion and, in doing so, a new, interesting detail came to light. A detail that he couldn't be sure of, but it nagged him and he had to pursue it.

As soon as he returned from his forty-minute outing with Charley, he dialed Alice Kramer's number. Although it was after 10 AM, a sleepy-voice answered the phone. Nick remembered that many senior residents had trouble sleeping and would stay up late, watching television or reading, and then, because they were retired and had no morning commitments, would sleep late. Alice was clearly in this group.

"Good morning, Alice. Sorry to bother you. It's Nick Dalton."

"Yes, Nick," came Alice's slow response.

Nick decided he wasn't going to jolt Alice into full consciousness by telling her about the parrot. Instead, he asked, "I know this may sound like a silly question but do you know if Emma's parrot greeted everyone with 'Hello, lady'?"

A pause on the other end and he could hear Alice's heavy breathing. Finally, in a voice still arising from sleep, she said, "Yes, Carlos greeted everyone who came to Emma's home."

"And did he always say the same thing: 'Hello Lady'?" Now his voice betrayed a note of urgency.

"Yes, I believe so."

"Even if it was a man or a woman?"

Alice's voice started to come alive. "Yes. No, wait a minute. I was there one day when Gillie came to fix something, and I believe Carlos greeted him differently."

"Was it 'Hello fella'?"

"Yes, that's right. That's what he said. I had never heard him say it before but that was the first time I was in Emma's home when a man came in, and I thought it was so cute. Then I heard him say it again when Carlton Wright came to see Emma just as I was leaving."

This was a new piece of information that Nick seized upon. "Was Carlton a friend of Emma's?"

"Not really!" Alice's voice sank to a confidential tone. "Between you and me, Emma was very upset about the conflict with her daughter over moving to a nursing home. They were really estranged and I believe Emma was seeking Carlton's professional help in dealing with the situation. I know he visited her several times."

"Did you mention this to Detective Grimes?" Nick asked.

Another pause as Alice sifted through her memory bank. "You know, I don't believe I did. But what bearing could that have on anything to do with her...with her death?" Her voice rose in alarm.

"Probably nothing," Nick said quickly, hoping to soothe her.

"Should I call the detective?" she asked, and Nick could sense her confusion.

"No need. I'll be speaking with him today and I'll mention it. It's just a detail, but he likes to know all the details. Leave it to me."

"Thank you, Nick," Alice said with genuine relief in her tone. "I've got to get myself together and get over to clean Carlos's cage."

Nick was now forced to tell Alice about Carlos.

"Oh dear!" Alice exclaimed, her voice shaking. "The poor, innocent creature! Who would have done this? And why?"

Nick realized that Alice was disassociating Emma's death with the death of the bird, and he had no desire to increase this lady's fright. "It might have been an accident." He said lamely, improvising on the spot. "Someone might have taken it out of its cage to play with it and got too rough."

This sounded as convincing to Nick as if he had said that the parrot was a secret CIA agent and had been rubbed out by the Russian KGB, but all Alice said was "How sad!" Nick decided to let sleeping dogs—or dead parrots—lie.

"I'll give it a proper burial," Alice said.

"That would be nice," responded Nick and they said goodbye.

Why, Nick asked himself, did Carlton Wright keep popping up in unexpected places, like the pool just before the parrot was killed, and then observed by Helen as walking quickly to his townhouse shortly after the dead bird was discovered, and now with Alice's surprising report that he had been visiting Emma more than once in her home? He made a mental note to share these troubling details with Jonathan.

22

Nick was dialing Jonathan's cell phone number when his doorbell rang. Reluctantly, he put the phone down and went to the door, silently cursing the community architect or the contractor for not putting peepholes in the front doors. No matter who was standing on his porch, it was always a surprise. This time, when he opened the door, it was a most unpleasant surprise.

Microphone in hand, a solemn looking Vienna Campos stood squarely in front of the door, while Nick saw a two-man television crew a few feet behind her in his walkway, their camera already rolling. Nick was taking in this scene when Vienna started talking.

"Mr. Dalton, can you give us any new information on the murder of Emma Craig?"

"No, I can't," Nick responded evenly, determined not to give the television reporter the least bit of information that could sensationalize Emma's death any further.

"Is it true that Fran Walker, the president of your Board of Managers, has disappeared and no one knows where she is?"

Again, in a calm voice and giving Vienna his best steady gaze, Nick said, "Ms. Walker is out of town attending to a very sick relative."

"Do you know exactly where she is?"

"She's caring for her sister."

"Exactly where is that?"

"In Oregon."

The microphone was bobbing between Vienna and Nick's faces like a Ping-Pong ball in a hot game.

"But where in Oregon?"

Vienna was relentless but Nick was resolute.

"That's private."

"Have you spoken with her since her mysterious departure?"

"There was nothing mysterious about her departure. I've told you the reason for it. "

"Is she a suspect in Emma Craig's murder?"

Nick took a deep breath, hoping to calm the rising agitation he was feeling with the third degree Vienna was giving him. "You'd have to ask the police," he said quietly.

Vienna switched topics. "As the vice president of the Board of Managers, what steps are you and your fellow Board members taking to assure the residents of Marsden Grove that they are safe in their homes?"

"The police have assigned extra patrols to the perimeter and our security guard is on high alert. Residents have been reminded to lock their doors. Detective Grimes, who is assigned to this case, has asked them to be alert and report to him anything they might see that seems suspicious or any detail they might remember about the time surrounding Mrs. Craig's death."

"Is it true that residents are arming themselves with guns?"

Nick blinked. Here was a question from left field, guaranteed to grab the attention of television viewers while watching the six o'clock local news. "I know of no such thing," he responded firmly.

"But I just spoke to another member of your Board of Managers, Mr. John Stevens, who retired as a major in the United States Marines, and he told me that fear was rampant across the community and he was pretty sure the killer of Mrs. Craig was a fellow resident, and the only way all the residents could protect themselves was to be armed."

Nick hoped he was concealing his rage when replying, "That's one man's opinion, and Mr. Stevens was not speaking for the Board."

"So are you saying that Mr. Stevens was wrong and residents are not buying guns?"

Nick spoke slowly while giving Vienna his steeliest gaze. "I told you what the police and the community's administration are doing. I have no knowledge of what individual residents are doing, but I will continue to advise them to be calm and let the police handle the matter. On this subject I can say nothing more."

Vienna started to ask another question just as Nick, giving her a phony smile, said "Have a nice day," stepped back and closed the door.

He stood behind the door and could feel his pulse racing. No doubt about it, she was a smart, aggressive reporter, he thought, eager to manipulate information and ferret out inconsistencies for their shock value. Unflinchingly, she went for the jugular. Then his thoughts turned to Major Whack-a-do and his big, uncontrollable mouth.

Suddenly, from outside the door he heard Vienna Campos's voice, giving her summation for the television camera.

"Marsden Grove is a community in turmoil as death stalks its pristine townhouses and tree-lined lanes, and senior citizens wait and watch, fearful of what might happen next. The Board of Managers seems to be in total disarray. The president has vanished to parts unknown and the vice president, as you have just seen, disagrees with his fellow Board member. The police seem no closer to solving the murder of Emma Craig, but the circumstances of her death suggest that it very likely could be a neighbor—some neighbor who harbored a deep grudge and a killer instinct and who, according to Rosemary Craig, Mrs. Craig's only daughter, sent Mrs. Craig a threatening note before striking and ending her life.'

Vienna paused, and when she spoke again, her voice rose in pitch. "Where is the missing president of the Board? Why are the Board members squabbling over how to protect the community? What was the motivation of this sadistic killer? Will the police solve this murder? Will Marsden Grove ever return to the peaceful, secure senior community it was? Or will fear and distrust take up permanent residence in this upscale enclave where people can no longer feel safe? And, worst of all, could this killer strike again? I will report on all updates to this baffling case as they unfold. This is Vienna Campos for WBIX News."

Nick stood transfixed behind the door, seething with rage at this dismal and forbidding picture of Marsden Grove that Vienna was bringing to the larger television audience, not to mention the devastating effect this reporting would have in inflaming the worst fears of all his fellow residents.

Once again his thoughts turned to the Major and his rage increased. Without moving, he waited until he heard the television van drive away. Then he was out the door and running toward the Major's townhouse, so easy to spot because of not one but two American flags, waving from both levels of the Major's home. Nick pushed the bell and heard the Marine anthem resonating inside while he simultaneously pounded on the door in a white fury.

When the Major answered the door, he registered a surprised look for only a second before Nick sunk his fingers around the Major's throat, shoved him backwards into his foyer, kicked the door closed with his foot and pushed the Major against the nearest wall, never releasing his powerful grip on the startled man's throat.

The Major's knees buckled, giving Nick's five-inch-height advantage even further sway. The contempt in Nick's eyes and the menace in his voice were further inducements to fear. Nick's words came fast, as though each one were being spit out with total revulsion.

"Listen to me, you god-damn tin soldier, you say one more word to any reporter and I guarantee there will be another murder in Marsden Grove and it will be yours. And it won't be neat and pretty because I'll tear you apart, limb by limb. Now shut your fuckin' mouth about the murder to anyone! No more military drills! No more call to arms? No more statements to the press! No more nothing!"

Nick was punctuating his demands with an ever-tighter squeeze on the Major's throat. His eyes bulging, his mouth sucking in air frantically, the Major looked on the verge of collapse, or at least of losing control of his bowels.

"Got it?" Nick asked in a half-hiss. The Major gurgled some sound as his Adam's apple quivered beneath Nick's taut grip. Unable to move his head, the Major battered his eyes in what Nick took to be his assent.

Nick released his grip and the Major sank to his knees, coughing and sucking in air noisily. Nick was out the door in a second and raced back to his home, feeling his anger dissipate with each rapid stride. If that doesn't keep the son of a bitch quiet, nothing will, he thought. As he opened the front door, panting from all his physical and emotional exertions, he heard his phone ringing and rushed to answer it, thinking it might be Jonathan.

23

As soon as Nick said "Hello," he heard Jonathan's voice. With no preamble, Jonathan said, "Your man Gillie is full of new information."

"Is it helpful?"

"Well, it sure as hell muddies the water some more. Gillie is now reporting that his master key to all the Marsden Grove homes was missing from his office for a few days, during the time of Emma's murder."

"Jesus!" Nick exclaimed. "How does he account for that?"

"He swears he always kept the master key in a locked drawer in his desk, but somehow it went missing and then a few days later he found it on the floor by his desk, so he didn't give it much thought."

Nick was quick with a response. "He probably was hitting the sauce and thought he might have dropped it unintentionally instead of putting it in the locked drawer."

"I asked him if that was a possibility. I told him I knew about his little problem but he looked scared and got very agitated and said he wasn't drinking at the time. I think he's scared of being fired."

Nick was seeing a pattern. "It seems as if everything we know surrounding Emma's murder—Gillie's seeing the tall, thin, shrouded person and the missing master key that could explain how the murderer got into Emma's home—all hinge on the accuracy and sobriety of our handy man."

"Where is his office and is it locked?"

"It's in the building that houses the recreation room and gym, next to the pool. And, no, it's not locked during the day since Gillie is always in and out, attending to the residents' emergencies and calls for help. It's only locked at night after Gillie leaves for the day."

"Does anyone else have a key to his office?"

"I think Fran Walker does, but I'll be damned if I know where she keeps it." Nick's annoyance was clear in his voice. "Her disappearing act was so sudden and fast that I never got a chance to go over any details with her."

"Nobody else?"

"Not that I know," Nick said, before starting down a tunnel of thoughts. "Either Gillie, in a drunken haze, didn't put the key back in the locked drawer and found it days later on the floor by his desk, or it was taken from his desk by somebody who used it to gain access to Emma's home. But Gillie kept the key in a locked drawer and he didn't mention any visible tampering with the lock, did he?"

"No, I asked him about that possibility and he swears, no. Now here's where Gillie throws me another curve."

Nick waited expectantly while Jonathan paused.

"I told Gillie I wanted to see his office and he appeared very anxious and admitted that there was a bottle of whiskey in the locked drawer where the master key is kept. He swears the bottle appeared on his desk two days before Emma's death, gift wrapped and with a typed note saying, 'Thanks for all your help.' Is Gillie allowed to do private jobs for the residents on the side?"

"Yes, we permit that, because the residents like and trust him and he does fine work. The only restriction is, he can't do any side jobs on community time, and, to my knowledge, he's always abided by that rule. Why?"

"I asked him who he thought the whiskey might have come from. He hesitated but then he said it might have come from Dr. Wright because he had just finished installing a new countertop for him. He admitted that he had consumed most of the bottle in the next few days, so that could account for a lot of slip-ups like dropping the master key on the floor or forgetting to lock the drawer."

Nick's response came quickly. "Jonathan, Carlton Wright keeps popping up everywhere in what could be considered suspicious circumstances. This morning, while I was in the gym, I heard Emma's parrot—Alice Kramer had placed the bird and his cage in the recreation room with a sign saying adoption for free—the parrot was screeching at the top of its lungs, screaming 'Carlos scared!' over and over. I ran into the recreation room and took one look at the frightened bird and realized it had probably seen the person who killed Emma. Remember, that was what the bird kept repeating for days after Emma's death. I ran out to the pool and found Susan Moriarity in the ladies room and she said Carlton Wright had just finished his morning swim. While I was talking to Susan, someone entered the gym from the outside entrance and then went into the recreation room through the gym's rear entrance and strangled the bird. A short while later, Helen Parker, my gym partner, returned from a jog and reported seeing Carlton hurrying to his townhouse. When I had originally passed through the recreation room on my shortcut to the gym, the parrot was very calm and greeted me with 'Hello fella.' When I got back home after discovering the dead parrot, I called Alice Kramer and she verified that she had heard the bird greet Gillie with 'Hello fella,' while he always said 'Hello lady' to any woman who visited Emma."

Jonathan was now thinking aloud. "Then Emma's murderer could have been a woman, except that, according to Gillie, the person he saw was shrouded in a hood, so Carlos could have been mistaken."

"Yes, that's possible," Nick admitted. "But here's another interesting piece of information that Alice mentioned. It seems that Emma was distraught over her estrangement from her daughter Rosemary and was seeking Carlton Wright's professional help in dealing with the situation, so he was coming to her home quite often."

Nick now waited for Jonathan's response.

"So our only eye-witness to Emma's murder is a parrot who's now dead. Carlton's connection to Emma and his appearance around the time the parrot was killed is strictly circumstantial, and Gillie's assumption that the whiskey that sent him off on a bender was from Carlton is just that—an assumption—and any decent lawyer could easily defend against these coincidences.

Nick realized that from his many years of experience probably testifying at trials, Jonathan was weighing aloud the flimsiness of the evidence against Carlton.

"Still," Jonathan continued, "he deserves watching and I'll check further into his background."

Nick had reported all his latest news and thought that Jonathan would make one of his abrupt endings. Instead, Jonathan said, "Here's a new twist to our story. Gillie told me that yesterday the security guard reported a break in the perimeter fence around Marsden Grove. He discovered it last night when he was responding to a resident's complaint about someone lurking in the bushes behind her townhouse. You only have one security guard, right?" A kid named Garth Hodgkiss."

"Yes, that's right. He's a college student and wants to be a cop after he graduates. A great kid and straight as an arrow. Very conscientious and shows great patience with us seniors and all our imagined prowlers. He's a hell of a lot more patient and indulgent with us than I was at his age."

"Yeah, he impressed me, too. He told me about wanting to be a cop when I interviewed him the night after Emma's body was discovered. Since the gap in the fence was hidden behind heavy shrubbery, we don't know how long it's been there or if it has any possible connection to Emma's murder."

"Jonathan, I just remembered something else. After I discovered the dead parrot I rushed outside through the front entrance of the gym and saw a white handkerchief dangling from a shrub along the path leading to the road. I carefully put it in a plastic baggy. I don't know if it could give up any evidence but I'll drop it off at the station later today."

"Thanks, Nick," was all Jonathan said, and there was a pause before he added, "You're a big help."

Nick thought for a moment that Jonathan was being sarcastic since no matter what Nick shared with the detective, Emma's murder was no nearer to solving. Then he heard Jonathan say, "I really appreciate it," and he knew that Jonathan was being sincere.

When Nick was in Vietnam, facing death every day, the reasons for war and the politics of war and the patriotic slogans surrounding war, all faded to nothingness, leaving a void that left him with only one motivation to fight: the band of brothers in his camp who became his family and who, like him, felt fierce allegiance only to their fighting comrades, to covering their flanks and buoying their collective spirits. Jonathan, too, had been in Vietnam, and while the challenge of solving Emma's death was not comparable to what they had faced in Nam, their joining forces in finding the murderer somehow, to Nick's thinking, established a special bond that only the two of them shared.

"Gotta go!" Jonathan announced. "Rosemary Craig wants to see me. Says it's urgent. Probably wants to sue the police for not finding her mother's murderer, and maybe she wants to slap Marsden Grove with a suit, too, for not keeping her mother safe. Who knows? People are slap-happy these days when it comes to law suits and the chance to make a quick buck. Plus, they expect miracles from the men in blue. Maybe I'll be seeing you in court, partner."

Nick was smiling when he said goodbye.

24

Nick had wanted to celebrate the thirty-fourth birthday of his son Tom with a dinner at The Cooked Goose in Amagansett, the restaurant where he and Judy and Tom had celebrated many family birthdays. But Christina had suggested a home-cooked meal and celebration at her house for Nick, Tom and Vera, Tom's wife. Knowing what a good cook Christina was and what meticulous care she took in preparing for special occasions, he happily agreed.

Since he was so smitten with Christina and, in the back of his mind, kept hoping that at some future time she might relent and agree to marry him, he wanted his only son and daughter-in-law to get to know Christina fully and see why he was so very happy with this new lady in his life.

On the previous occasions when Nick had arranged for the four of them to get together, things had gone extremely well. Tom and Vera were both easy-going, unpretentious people, and Nick was grateful that Tom seemed to accept Christina with no umbrage that she was taking

Judy's place in Nick's life. For her part, Christina quickly became friends with Vera and always respected the special bond between father and son without ever trying to insinuate herself into that personal realm.

As he could have predicted, Christina took special care to make Tom's birthday a festive occasion, including a delicious multi-course, home-made dinner featuring many of Tom's favorite dishes, about which she had grilled Nick in advance, a beautifully decorated birthday cake with buttercream icing, Tom's favorite, and a hand-made banner saying, "Happy 34th Birthday, Tom."

They drank champagne that Nick had brought and sampled several tasty hors d'oeuvres that Christina and Vera had prepared together. Talk and laughter flowed easily, including steady father-son japes. After dinner, when Tom and Nick had finished their second helpings, Christina lit the candles on the birthday cake, turned off the lights and led Nick and Vera in a rousing chorus of the Happy Birthday song.

The evening had been the perfect antidote to all the pressures Nick had been feeling over the mystery of Emma Craig's death and the resulting tumult at Marsden Grove. The party continued until nearly eleven when Tom and Vera, with hugs and thanks all around, said their good nights and departed.

Refreshed and relaxed, Nick helped Christina clean up, always impressed with how well they worked together, intuitively and effortlessly. In a giddy mood, Nick started whistling the Disney tune, Whistle While you Work, from the movie *Snow White and the Seven Dwarfs*. Christina laughed when she caught the tune but soon she joined in by singing the song's lyrics. Tom started banging on a pot he had been drying while Christina accompanied him on two spoons.

Their intimate, lighthearted mood was broken by the ringing of Nick's cell phone.

"Who would be calling me at this hour?" he asked, dismayed that their spell was abruptly ended. He glanced at the incoming number and recognized it as Jonathan's. Still he answered with a curt "Yes?"

"Sorry to bother you," Jonathan said, "but I thought you should know. Rosemary Craig was found drowned in her own pool about an hour ago."

Stunned into silence, Nick made no response as his mind fumbled in taking in this astonishing news.

Filling the void, Jonathan said, "Her neighbor discovered her floating body when she went to investigate why Rosemary's dog, who's usually very quiet, kept barking."

"Was there any evidence of foul play?" Nick asked, finally commanding his mind to focus.

"Can't tell for sure. We'll have to wait for the coroner's report. The body's been removed and I've requested a speedy report."

"Are you there now?"

"Yeah, but I'm just wrapping things up. The only detail that's immediately suspicious is the gate to the pool and back yard was found open when the neighbor arrived. He told me that Rosemary's dog was a wanderer and she always kept that gate closed. The neighbor found the dog by the side of the pool, nearest to Rosemary's body. The dog sensed something was wrong and didn't wander off this time. Just kept barking to get someone's attention."

Nick thought of Charley's uncanny ability to intuit Nick's moods and saw in what Jonathan was describing another example of a dog's capacity for love and loyalty and sensing when something was amiss.

"A damn fine dog!" Jonathan remarked. "A yellow lab, male."

"Jonathan, is this just some horrendous coincidence or is someone out to kill off the family and now they've succeeded?" Nick's voice rose in pitch as he asked this question, so frightening were its implications.

"Don't know yet," Jonathan replied, "but it is a staggering coincidence. I'll touch base with you tomorrow."

Nick's previous speculation about the special bond he and Jonathan had formed was now, he reflected, confirmed. Why else did Jonathan feel the need to call Nick immediately with the news of Rosemary's death and not wait until tomorrow? Jonathan wanted to share this news with the one person he trusted and respected. It was like back in Nam when Nick returned from a sortie, flying over the Ho Chi Minh Trail, and had to immediately tell his buddies everything that had happened in order to decompress. He and Jonathan were now a band of two brothers and Nick resolved to do everything he could to help his brother.

Nick was too preoccupied for any love-making that night. Christina wordlessly seemed to understand. They fell asleep wrapped in each other's arms, but Nick had troubled dreams of riots at Marsden Grove, as seniors armed to the teeth took pot-shots at anything and anybody. Even the ones with walkers carried their guns in shoulder holsters and steadied their aim on the bars of their walkers.

He woke in a cold sweat and lay awake, listening to the soft rhythmic breathing of Christina, snuggled against his side, as he endlessly pondered the burning question: Was Rosemary's death some ridiculous coincidence or was this another murder made to look like an accident? And if it was murder, what was the killer's motivation? His mind drifted back to the common thread surrounding the death of Emma and, earlier, her sister in Pennsylvania: the note about sins of the past.

Nick suddenly recalled that Rosemary had left a message yesterday for Jonathan, stressing the urgent need to speak to him. Did Jonathan get back to her and learn her urgent news? The detective hadn't mentioned it in his brief call announcing Rosemary's death. Perhaps there were other people within earshot and he wanted to share the news only with Nick.

Unresolved issues, perplexing questions, mounting pressure, all left Nick in a state of sleepless dread.

25

The next morning Nick slept late, after finally falling back to sleep just as dawn was breaking. Upon waking, he was greeted by a smiling Christina and a tail-whipping Charley, who had made himself just as comfortable in Christina's home as in his own.

After a hearty breakfast prepared by the ever-attentive Christina and a walk with Charley, Nick returned to Marsden Grove and found bedlam. He had no sooner passed the electronic entrance gate and was obeying the twenty-mile speed limit when he was flagged down by a clearly excited Jack Moriarity, waving a newspaper. Nick stopped and Jack started talking immediately.

"Have you seen this morning's paper?"

Before Nick could utter a word, Jack unfolded the paper and thrust it inside the car. Nick read the headline of the local paper: Daughter of Marsden Grove Murder Victim Mysteriously Found Drowned

"They had to add 'mysteriously,'" Nick said aloud, his temples starting to twitch.

"Everybody here is alarmed," Jack said. "Talking about moving or buying guns."

"That's all we need: an armed camp!" Nick responded, with annoyance punctuating his words. "Half the residents have such poor vision, they'd probably shoot their nearest neighbor, mistaking him or her for a prowler."

Jack looked quizzically at Nick. "Then you've already heard?"

"Heard what?"

"The Major saw someone skulking around the bushes about five this morning and thinking it was the killer, got out his military-issued pistol and shot the guy in the leg."

"Jesus Christ!" Nick exploded, feeling like Alice in Wonderland, falling down the rabbit hole into Bizzaro-Land. "Who the hell did he hit?"

Jack displayed a sly grin. "He shot Henry Cushman who was sneaking back to his home having spent the night with Violet Tomby. Everybody knows they're shacking up and trying to keep it on the QT. Still, it's just adding fuel to the fire and rattling all the seniors. As soon as they heard the shot, they started calling the security guard or 911 and some of them just stuck their heads out of their windows and screamed for help. Nerves are frayed to the breaking point."

Nick nodded in agreement. "Is Henry okay?"

"Yeah, just a flesh wound in the calf. But Violet is hysterical, whether from having her boyfriend shot or from having their affair out in the open now, I couldn't say."

Nick thanked Jack and drove to his townhouse where he found Jonathan's unmarked sedan in his driveway. Reminiscent of the first time Nick saw Jonathan, the detective was casually leaning against the fender of his car, smoking a cigarette.

"Don't you know they're bad for you?" Nick chided, alighting from his car as Charley bounded over to Jonathan and got a welcomed scratch behind the ears.

"We're all goin', one way or another," Jonathan said, smiling and continuing to scratch Charley.

"Yeah, but smoking's a guaranteed exit ramp," Nick said, but in a light, bantering tone.

"It's my only vice," Jonathan responded, throwing up his arms in mock defense.

Nick led the way into his townhouse followed by Jonathan and Charley. He quickly glanced at his message machine and saw eleven new messages.

"One of those is mine," Jonathan said, seeing Nick pause before the answering machine. "I called you earlier at Christina's and she told me you were on your way home."

Nick shook his head. "I just can't deal with this right now," he said emphatically, anticipating all the alarm and wild charges and demands from hysterical residents in those phone messages.

"Want to grab an early lunch?" Jonathan offered, not unsympathetically.

Nick glanced at his watch and saw it was eleven-thirty. "I had a late, big breakfast but I'll join you in a beer," he said, pleased that this would be the first time he and Jonathan had any kind of social interaction.

"We'll go to a place I know two towns over, where we can talk and won't be disturbed," Jonathan said, heading back toward the front door.

Upon seeing his master heading out again, Charley was eager to join him. "You stay, Charley," was Nick's soft command, and Charley, his disappointment reflected in a few whimpers of protest, watched the front door close before retreating to his big cushion and settling in for a snooze.

They drove in Jonathan's car to a bar and restaurant about thirty minutes away from Marsden Grove. The place was dark with a worn, slightly musty smell and a lot of cops in uniform on a lunch break. Jonathan greeted several by name as he led Nick to a booth in an isolated corner. "We can talk here," he said, sliding into the booth, with Nick quickly following on the opposite side. "I know you said you weren't hungry but their burgers are outstanding."

A middle-age waitress, who breezily addressed Jonathan by his first name and whom Jonathan called Dolly, took their orders: a Coors Light and a mushroom-cheese burger for Jonathan and, succumbing to Jonathan's praise, a plain burger with onions and another Coors Light for Nick.

"A popular place with the men in blue!" Nick remarked as Dolly walked away.

"It's owned by three retired cops so we're very comfortable here," Jonathan explained.

"And I am, too, with all the fire power protecting me!" Nick said. Both men laughed.

While waiting for their food, Nick asked, "So, are you still taking care of your grandkids?" His question was tentative for he was eager to learn about Jonathan's family but didn't know if this was a line Jonathan wouldn't let him cross. He was relieved to see Jonathan smile

"No, their parents returned yesterday. It was only a week's cruise in the Caribbean. The kids were away at day camp and my other daughter, Jessie, came around at night to help out with them"

"How many kids do you have?" Nick asked, hoping again that Jonathan would not find his question intrusive.

"Just two: Kathleen, the married one, the mother of Samantha and Eric, and Jessie, who's an out-and-proud lesbian."

Jonathan gave Nick one of his steely-eyed searches to gauge Nick's response to this last statement, but Nick didn't flinch. "Thanks to all the LGBT's being out and proud, we're witnessing a huge cultural change," he said, smiling with conviction.

Jonathan returned Nick's smile. "Yeah, it's a hell of a different world than when we grew up. It takes a lot of getting used to, but I suppose it's all for the best."

"At least they no longer have to hide and try to live a lie," Nick said. "We had this pilot in my group in Nam—the biggest, toughest, most macho guy you ever met, always talking about all his girl friends back home and how many women he'd laid—anyway, a bunch of us had a reunion ten years later and he shows up with a big dude who looks even tougher than him and proudly introduces him as his life partner. We all got smashed and started letting our guard down, and he admitted that he felt trapped in the closet, had gone through two disastrous marriages and thought seriously about suicide all the time before he decided to come out. Now he had accepted who he is and was very happy with his partner and anyone who didn't like it could go fuck themselves."

Jonathan had listened intently to Nick's narrative and now responded. "It's interesting how the old stereotypes of gays and lesbians have broken down. My daughter Jessie is the most feminine woman you could imagine. Always fussin' with her make-up and hair and really into clothes and shopping. Like that macho pilot you described, she doesn't fit the old mold. But they know who they are and they won't pretend otherwise. You have to admire that. Hell, we even have openly gay cops now. That takes guts!"

Nick shook his head in agreement, then asked, "How does your wife feel about it?"

"Which wife?" Jonathan asked abruptly.

Surprised, Nick hesitated before saying, "Jessie's mother."

Jonathan still revealed a half-smile as he looked away from Nick and played with the salt and pepper shakers. "Jessie's mother, the mother of my only children, was my first wife. We were high school sweethearts, got married still in our teens and hated each other by our mid-twenties. She had no motherly instincts and blamed me for forcing her to have children. We split and she took off for parts unknown, giving me full custody of the girls."

"That must have been rough on you," Nick interjected.

"Really rough!" Jonathan said, his voice tinged with anger. "I quickly found a woman I thought would be a good mother to my kids and remarried less than a year after my divorce. Unfortunately, wife-number-two did love kids but she also loved booze, and when she was drunk, you never knew who would turn up: Mary Poppins or Cinderella's stepmother. Once I caught her in a drunken rage slapping my girls around and that was the end of that marriage. From then on, I hired live-in housekeepers with maternal instincts and kept my lady friends on the side."

Jonathan's marital history had been delivered in a low, even tone, like some interior monologue. Then, as if returning from a reverie, he stopped fingering the shakers, let his shoulders sink against the back of the booth and again looked squarely at Nick.

"Now that the kids are grown, I have a steady lady in my life, Mary Lou, but she's got three grown children, all with problems, and siblings she's always battling with, and I've got strange hours with my work, so we've agreed to live apart and keep our time together special. We go on vacations and spend weekends away, and we're both happy with what we've got. Sometimes I think it would be nice to have the daily intimacy of a full-time wife, but then I remember my track record and begin to think that 'happily ever after' is a fantasy, or just not for me."

Dolly delivered the burgers and beer along with a few pleasant exchanges with Jonathan, and the men ate in silence, except for Nick's remarking on the outstanding quality of his burger. The burgers came with a plateful of

French fries and these, too, Nick found deliciously seasoned.

"Told you so," was all Jonathan said to Nick's exclamations of gustatory delight.   Nick made a mental note to bring Christina here, especially since she loved a good hamburger.

Over coffee, at Jonathan's prompting, Nick gave a brief history of his happy life with Judy and now his good fortune in finding Christina. He described the warmth of last night's celebration of his son Tom's birthday.

"You obviously caught the gold ring on the marriage merry-go-round.   Lucky you!" was Jonathan's conclusion when Nick had finished.

"I think I could catch it twice if Christina ever consented to marry me," Nick said, and his frustration was evident.

"Give her time," Jonathan advised.

They ordered coffee refills, and, in a momentary silence that was neither forced nor awkward, Nick thought back to the shared histories the men in his group in Nam had enjoyed as part of their bonding process. He was pleased that he and Jonathan had now shared some of their personal stories as further evidence of their growing fellowship.   His pleasant reflections were interrupted when Jonathan, taking a final gulp of his coffee and placing his mug decisively on the table, said, "Okay, down to business!" Nick was instantly alert.

"First of all," Jonathan began, "the handkerchief. The lab found the fingerprints of Susan Moriarity on it. But since you told me that she was with you outside the recreation room when the parrot was killed, that leaves her out. I think it probably belongs to her and she dropped it on leaving the gym. Didn't you say she was suffering from the runs?"

Nick nodded.

"I checked on Carlton Wright and he's clean. Yale PH.D., a widower like you, no skirmishes with the law. I know he keeps turning up at suspicious places but my gut feeling is, it's just coincidence and he's not a hot prospect."

Nick nodded again.

"Now let's get to the big items. I don't believe Rosemary Craig drowned!"

Nick blinked several times at this jarring declaration before asking, "What makes you think that?"

Jonathan was quick to respond. "Because I saw the body and what I didn't mention on the phone last night because there were people standing around was that there were bruises on the back of Rosemary's neck clearly visible since she wore her hair very short. I think she was swimming in her pool when somebody came into the gated yard, jumped in the pool and pushed Rosemary's head under water."

"Wouldn't that have taken a lot of strength? Rosemary would have fought."

"Yeah, but the element of surprise would have caused panic and while fighting in a state of total panic, realizing someone was trying to kill her, she would have consumed her limited supply of oxygen more quickly, even involuntarily opening her mouth to scream and letting water in. Consciousness would have slipped away in less than a few minutes and the deed was done."

"What about her dog?" Nick asked.

"The dog is very friendly and not a guard dog at all. He might have thought the killer was just playing with Rosemary, you know, roughhousing in the water. The killer hurried away without closing the gate. When Rosemary didn't move, the dog sensed something was wrong and started barking. The coroner's report won't be out for a while but I know it will support my conclusion."

Nick's thoughts were reeling. "So now we have two murders and no clear suspects, no clues and no witnesses except a now dead parrot and a barking dog," he said, despair in his voice.

Jonathan paused and reached inside his jacket. "No particular suspects but some more clues," he announced sternly, extricating a bulky manila envelope and placing its contents on the table. Nick surveyed a small book and a single piece of crumpled paper.

Jonathan picked up the paper, unfolded it and pushed it across the table to Nick. "I found this while going through Rosemary's trash." In bold, black printed letters were four words: SINS OF THE PAST.

Nick was laboring to make sense of them when Jonathan continued. "Remember how Emma's sister in Pennsylvania got a note threatening to expose some terrible secret of the past and then on that very night she was killed in a hit-and-run? And after Emma's death, Rosemary discovered a note sent to her mother saying 'You must pay for past sins.' So now the entire family is wiped out, all having received the same ominous note. There's something in this family's past that our killer is seeking revenge for. That's what caused the sister in Pennsylvania to change her name legally from Strelitz to Steele and perhaps that's also why Emma and her sister never communicated and Rosemary didn't even know her mother had a sister. Emma married, so her name automatically changed."

Nick interrupted Jonathan. "If we could find something in the history of Emma and her sister that might cause someone to seek revenge, that would be a big help, right?"

Jonathan smiled indulgently. "Only if we could connect that history to someone in the present."

Nick added, "And, given the ages of Emma and her sister, we don't know how far back in the past to look."

"There I think we have a clue. The records show that Emma's sister changed her name officially shortly after her father's suicide and Emma's marriage a few months later, so that tells us it was around 1950."

Nick's mind was racing. "Could the father's suicide be another murder made to look like a suicide?"

"No," Jonathan responded. "The man jumped off the George Washington Bridge and witnesses saw him rush from his car and leap over the railing. But we don't know if his suicide was also the result of someone's threatening to reveal some horrible 'past sin.'"

"But wouldn't that lead us back to Germany and a dead end?"

"Most likely," Jonathan agreed before adding, "But still there has to be some connection between the far distant past and the present. If we find that connection, we might find our killer."

Jonathan now picked up the small book from the table and opened it to a particular page. "This is Emma's diary. Rosemary found it hidden in the back of Emma's desk and that's when she placed the urgent call to me."

Handing the diary to Nick with his thumb marking the page, Jonathan said, "Rea this!"

Nick had to adjust his eyes to the small, carefully executed handwriting, but then he noted the date of the entry as being approximately six months before the current date. He read.

"The parrot was a lovely surprise gift, left on my doorstep with a note saying his name was Carlos and he was very friendly and would give me much joy and companionship. It was signed 'a secret admirer.' I couldn't leave the bird on the doorstep and he does keep my company with all his chattering, but lately, among his many words and phrases, he repeats one from The

Lord's Prayer, 'forgive us our sins,' that sends shivers through me, given what my sister experienced just before she died. Am I making too much of this or is this some implied threat?"

Nick finished reading this passage and handed the diary back to Jonathan before commenting, "The sisters must have been in secret communication without Rosemary's knowledge."

"Emma's phone records show that," Jonathan said, turning the diary to another page while saying, "This was Emma's last entry before she was killed."

Nick read again.

"The note arrived today, stuck under my door when I got up this morning and went for my mail. There's no mistaking what it means. Someone knows. Someone has finally caught up to me, despite the changes I made to escape the past. I'm very frightened but I don't know what to do. If I went to the police, I'd have to explain everything about what I think the note is referring to, and that would be horrible, especially for Rosemary. And I can't even say who this person is who's on to the past. I'm scared to be alone, especially at night. If I can't sleep tonight, I'll call a friend."

Nick closed the diary and said, "I guess she didn't call a friend that night."

Jonathan was quick to respond. "Or maybe she called someone she thought was a friend and that person killed her. That's one possibility. The other possibility is that someone stole the master key from Gillie's desk and used it to gain entry to Emma's townhouse and strangled her while she slept."

"Just to add to the confusion," Nick said, "since the hole in the perimeter fencing was discovered and we don't know how long it was there or who made it, we can't really confine our suspects to the residents at Marsden Grove. If the killer was masquerading as a friend, it could have been a friend from the community or from the town." Defeat was clearly implied in Nick's tone. "Meantime I've got the Major shooting another resident, mistaking him for a prowler and trying to be a hero."

"That was reported to me. He's got a permit for the gun."

"Okay, but now everyone's in a total panic, talking about moving and threatening to buy guns and clamoring for more protection."

"I know," Jonathan said. "We get lots of calls from your residents, demanding action, accusing other residents and asking advice on what guns they should buy. One lady asked if we could teach her how to use a machine gun, and a gentleman asked where he could buy a bazooka.

"They're out of control, in total free-fall!" Nick admitted. "And next Saturday we have another community meeting to elect a resident to the Board of Managers. Unfortunately our by-laws don't limit the number of terms a Board member can serve, so the Major is running again for a new five-year term and his opposition is Dagmar Neilson, our resident scold on all things environmental, and Sonia Arcadivich, our phony mystic and fortune teller. You should come just to see all the fireworks when the crazies butt heads. Next Saturday, 10 AM."

"Sorry, Nick, it's my grandson's birthday, and I'm taking the family to Hershey Park in Pennsylvania for the weekend. I'll touch base with you on Monday."

With the local newspaper headline announcing Rosemary Craig's drowning as being mysterious, this next community meeting, Nick reflected sourly, should reach new heights of hysteria and mayhem. For the hundredth time he cursed Fran Walker for her convenient disappearing act and momentarily thought about disappearing himself. His strong sense of duty dismissed this fleeting idea. The circus was again coming to town and he was the ringmaster, while two murders were unsolved and a killer was loose.

26

Saturday dawned hot and sultry, and the weather underscored the steamy turbulence of the Marsden Grove community as its residents gathered under the portable canvas cover to elect a representative to the Board of Managers. More importantly, they were there to enjoy a full-fledged venting of fear, frustration and hysteria over the unsolved murder of Emma Craig, whom most residents had now come to describe as one of their closest friends. To this anticipated emotional catharsis was added the extra dimension of her daughter's mysterious drowning, which had already been translated into another brutal murder by a bestial killer—even without knowing the evidence that Jonathan had shared exclusively with Nick, confirming foul play.

Elections to the Board were conducted in a typically American political way, with candidates announcing their intentions to run well in advance of the election date and then gathering support from among their fellow residents.

As Jonathan entered under the canvas cover, he saw large signs held aloft expressing support for each of the three candidates. The signs supporting Dagmar Neilson read, LOVE AND RESPECT MOTHER EARTH—VOTE FOR DAGMAR. Since Dagmar was so imperious and dictatorial in her quest for environmental conservancy, her followers were few but rabid.

A large group of female residents seemed to be behind Sonia Arcadivich's candidacy. Their signs said, TO THE FUTURE WITH SONIA. Nick chuckled as he thought of all the nebulous predictions Sonia usually made about the future—either something good or something bad—so that no matter what happened, she could hang her prediction on some small event, thereby reinforcing her reputation with the more gullible residents for clairvoyant powers.

Nick noted that even the Major had his followers, mostly veterans from WW II. Nick knew that many of these men had seen combat and survived harrowing experiences during their tours of duty, unlike the Major who held only safe desk jobs in the States. Yet, they bought his spit-and-polish, gung-ho image as a kindred spirit and mistook him as an exemplar of bravery and dedication to duty. Their signs said, LAW AND

ORDER WITH MAJOR JOHN, and A LEADER IN WAR, A LEADER IN PEACE—MAJOR JOHN.

The only leadership the Major might have provided in war or peace, Nick thought disdainfully, was directing the coffee wagon through his army offices. Nick thought a more suitable sign for the Major would be, HE'LL HUFF AND HE'LL PUFF BUT HE WON'T BLOW THE HOUSE DOWN. HE'LL ONLY BLOW SMOKE UP YOUR ASS.

Nick saw several other signs that reflected the views of a large group of residents.

WE DEMAND ACTION!

SOLVE THESE MURDERS!

LET US FEEL SAFE IN OUR HOMES AGAIN.

More lugubrious signs said WHO'S THE NEXT VICTIM? And one particularly wry sign said SOMEONE KNOWS WHO THE KILLER IS AND ISN'T TALKING. Yeah, Nick though, the killer!

The noise level was deafening as Nick took his place at a table facing the audience, sitting next to the three candidates. Despite the heat and oppressive humidity, the Major was in full-dress uniform and Sonia was covered in dark layers from head to foot as though she were embarking on a trek through the Ural Mountains. Nick glanced at Christina, sitting again with Helen Parker, and both gave him an encouraging smile.

Each candidate was allotted five minutes to present himself to the community and convince residents to support him/her, with Nick, in Fran Walker's absence, serving as moderator. The Major was sitting next to Nick, sweating profusely and studying copious notes. Nick leaned over and, in his most threatening voice, whispered in the Major's ear, "If you say anything about Emma Craig or her daughter that incites further agitation in this community, you will incite me to violence and all my violence will be directed against you. Remember that!"

Nick's words had an immediate effect on the Major who began rifling through his note cards and eliminating several from the pack.

Reverent Tom Schneider, or Reverend Pious as Nick privately referred to him, was slowly making his way through the crowd with his usual aura of pomposity, as though he were about to perform the miracle of the loaves and fishes for the multitudes. He approached Nick and solemnly announced, "I'll be happy to give a Convocation."

"That won't be necessary, Tom," Nick said quickly, barely concealing his disdain. "This is an election, not a revival meeting."

The Reverend was not to be deterred, having gained a modicum of fame within the community by self-publishing a book called *The Jesus Diet,* in which he offered a basic diet, lifted off the internet, and mingled that with daily reflections to bring your hearts and burdens—especially the excess burden your body might be carrying—to Jesus and seek His help in achieving a slimmer body and a more rigorous spiritual life.

Nick thought this combination was a clever gimmick that couldn't fail, in principle at least, because it offered the possibility of a better life both here and in the beyond. Many of Marsden Grove's ladies and a few of the gentlemen—who said they were buying it as gifts for overweight friends or relatives but who clearly were packing too many pounds, themselves—attended a book signing party at the Reverend's townhouse. If it weren't for Emma's murder and her daughter's drowning, the book would have gained much more buzz. Still, Reverend Pious now considered himself a celebrity author and felt he belonged front and center at all community events.

"It can't do any harm to ask our Lord and Savior's guidance in making our community decisions," he sanctimoniously intoned, but Nick wasn't having any of it. "I'm sure you have a direct line to the Lord, Tom, so you speak to him privately for those who believe in Him."

"Who doesn't believe in the Lord?" Tom asked with sheer bewilderment.

"Jews, Muslims, Buddhists, Shintoists, Zoroastrians, Rastafarians, pantheists, agnostics and atheists like me!" Nick said, rising from his seat and tapping the microphone on the lectern to be sure it was functioning.

"How sad! I'll pray for you," Tom proclaimed before melting back into the crowd.

Good morning, fellow residents," Nick said directly into the microphone in a loud voice to ensure attention. "We now have an important task to perform to guarantee the continued proper management of our community."

From somewhere in the audience Bill Russell, the retired New York City cop, shouted, "Not as important as finding a killer!" followed by shouts and murmurs of approval and some sporadic clapping.

"No one will want to move here!" wailed Vera Parks, desperate for a long time to sell her unit at an inflated price.

"Who could blame them? Would you?" someone shouted before adding sarcastically, "Enjoy your final years at Marsden Grove! No, make that your final hours! Our new slogan should be COME TO MARSDEN GROVE FOR ETERNAL PEACE."

Heads were shaking, the noise was rising and Nick could see the crowd gaining a full head of steam. Throwing all caution to the winds, with his patience totally exhausted, he shouted, "LISTEN UP! We are here today for one purpose only, and that is to elect a member to our Board of Managers, and that is what we are going to do! Otherwise, I'll call a halt to this meeting and we can all go home!"

"You don't have the authority to do that!" someone shouted.

"Do you want to come up here and take over the meeting?" Nick shot back and there was no response.

The Reverend Pious was on his feet. "I think we need a minute of silent prayer to bring us together."

Nick responded with, "I think we need a minute of silent sanity to refocus on our purpose here today."

Nick paused and, whether in prayer or silent reflection, the audience was now mostly silent, so Nick moved on. "Each candidate will have five minutes and no more to present his or her candidacy to the community. The candidates will speak in alphabetical order. Sonia Arcadivich is our first speaker."

Sonia rose from her seat slowly and stood silently behind the lectern as if she were communing with the spirit world. When she finally began to speak in her heavily accented, sepulchral voice, she spoke of nothing tangible, only mystical abstractions. How troubled voices must be heard. How fraught spirits must be soothed. How broken hearts must be mended. How a frightening future must be faced.

Nick thought at any moment she would predict the exact day and time of the Rapture and then start selling tickets to the Heavenly Express. She did everything but start speaking in tongues. She ended by inviting everyone to join her in the Circle of Life, a direct steal from *The Lion King*, but her entire flim-flam production seemed to be effective with any number of clapping, tear-stained ladies.

Next up was Dagmar Neilson, who launched into a listing of statistics, beginning with global deforestation and the gargantuan mountains of garbage polluting the planet. Then she referred to needless pollution of streams, rivers and estuaries in the county and finally turned her attention to Marsden Grove.

Up to this point Nick thought Dagmar had been impressive, for she was clearly knowledgeable and passionate about this subject, which merited attention, especially when the local economic incentive was not to recycle. But true to form, it wasn't what Dagmar said; it was the way she said it. For the last three minutes of her allotted time she harangued, browbeat, castigated, insulted, upbraided and caustically exhorted residents to take extraordinary measures to achieve total harmony with our environment. The glazed look on the faces of most audience members when she finished, said it all.

"Remember my warning!" Nick whispered to the Major before rising to announce the final speaker. Clearly rattled by Nick's overt threats and menacing stares, the Major kept shuffling his note cards, clearing his throat and, after starting to speak, stopping in mid-sentence and starting over.

It was obvious to Nick that the Major had hoped to ride to victory by extoling a strong law-and-order approach to all of Marsden Grove's problems, particularly Emma's murder. He must have written some incendiary passages about bringing a killer to justice, Nick thought, as the Major rambled on, shifting from one innocuous topic to another. Having been cowed by Nick's threats to exclude all references to murder, his main theme was lost and he was wandering hopelessly among inconsequential issues and talking repeatedly about the "hard work, countless hours and strong leadership" he had brought to the Board during his current term.

It took all of Nick's control to suppress a laugh when the "strong leadership" reference was made. The Major ended with a patriotic screed about devoting his life to the service of his country, and now to the citizens of Marsden Grove, and how proud he was to be in the greatest country in the world and "God bless America and God bless Marsden Grove and God bless all of you."

He forgot to bless the pets, Nick thought; then he remembered a passage from Macbeth: "a tale told by an idiot, full of sound and fury, signifying nothing."

Glumly, the Major, deprived of his personal sword-brandishing approach by Nick, returned to his seat. Nick quickly rose and announced that questions from the audience could now be addressed to individual candidates or all of the candidates. Several hands instantly floated up and Nick called on Ted Clark who together with his wife Amy were regarded by the community as alcoholics from all the liquor that was delivered to their townhouse. Ted spoke hesitantly. "I'd like to know what each of the candidates proposes to do to help the police catch Emma's killer."

The Major, seizing this opening, started to rise but was restrained by Nick's hand tightly gripping his arm. Nick responded in an authoritative voice.

"Every member of the current Board of Managers and any new member has one responsibility only, and that is to cooperate fully with Detective Grimes and the local police department in carrying out any requests they make of us. It would not be appropriate for one

Board member, or any candidate for the Board, to articulate some private plan beyond the mission we have been given by Detective Grimes: To be alert and to report anything unusual." Nick now raised his voice to a thunderous pitch. "This topic is unsuitable for further questions. Any other questions? Yes, Jack."

Jack Moriarity stood and with a broad grin asked, "Do you recommend we all get guns and start shooting anything that moves?"

"I'd be the first one he'd shoot!" Jack's wife Susan shouted out amidst titters and giggles, since no one knew if the battling Moriaritys should be taken seriously or if their endless battles were a strange form of love-play.

"You betcha. And I'd claim I thought you were a prowler," Jack said, still grinning.

"Who just happened to be lying in our own bed!" Susan shot back and now there was more open laughter.

Nick was quick to respond. "Given the unfortunate circumstances that can result from overanxious imaginations or poor eyesight, no, that's not recommended." He did a quick visual sweep of the audience and noted that the wounded Henry Cushman and the embarrassed Violet Tomby were both absent. The Major looked decidedly uncomfortable.   Good, Nick thought.

Other topics were raised for the candidates which Sonia only answered in mystical riddles, the Major managed to bring all his responses under the American flag and love for one's country, and Dagmar dismissed them as being insignificant compared to environmental concerns and the urgent need for recycling. These unresponsive answers, coupled with the stifling heat and Nick's interdiction on the topic of murder pervading the community, led to a speedy ending of the meeting.

27

Nick was heading quickly away from the gathering throngs clustered together after the meeting closed, with Christina at his side, when he was intercepted by Jane, the Cat Lady, holding an old-fashioned instamatic camera and asking him to pose for a picture. Reluctantly he stopped and managed a half-smile while squinting in the intense sunlight.

"I took some pictures before the meeting, Nick. I thought we could put them in our quarterly newsletter. Look them over and see what you think."

Nick thanked Jane perfunctorily, took the envelope with the pictures and proceeded towards home. With so many recent days of record heat and humidity, Nick had not played his usual rounds of golf or even taken Charley for as many extended romps through the Preserve. The heat sapped his energy and today was no exception. On arriving home he had taken Charley for a brief walk but even Charley seemed to slow down in the heat, and both dog and master were happy to quickly return to their air-conditioned home.

"Let's have a big salad for lunch," Christina suggested and Nick readily agreed. She handed him a tall glass of ice tea. "You relax while I make the salad." As much as he enjoyed working with Christina in the kitchen, he was happy to take his glass of ice tea and retreat to the family room's big leather chair.

He was deciding whether to watch one of the classic golf games on television when he remembered the pictures that the Cat Lady had given him. He retrieved the envelope from the bench in the foyer and returned to his favorite chair and started glancing through them.

That Jane was no whiz photographer was immediately apparent. She must have asked several residents to wave at the camera and they indulgently complied. There was a picture of Vera Parks with the battling Moriaritys, half-waving, half-shielding their eyes from the sun. Another picture had Helen Parker, his gym buddy, shyly looking directly at the camera but dutifully extending her arm up in a full wave.

The Reverend Tom Schneider, the pious one, didn't look so much as he was waving as he was blessing the crowd, and Alice Kramer must have been talking to Cat Lady when she was snapped because her mouth was fully open, making her resemble a guppy, and her hand was resting on her breast. Dagmar Neilson stood stiffly like an old-time circuit-riding judge, ready to dispense harsh sentences on all offenders, neither smiling nor waving. Mabel Thomas, the community flirt, was posing like some long-ago pin-up queen, her hand raising her skirt, displaying a flexed leg. With a broad wink and a wide-mouth smile, she looked as though she were trying to seduce the camera.

The best picture was of the Major, Nick thought, laughing aloud when he came upon it. There he was in rigid attention and full military regalia, barely five-and-one-half feet of self-inflated pomposity, arms hanging ramrod straight at his side, staring sternly into the distance like some general surveying the bloody beaches at Normandy.. With just a circle of rouge to the cheeks, Nick suddenly thought, he could take his place among the Rockettes at Radio City Music Hall's Christmas performance of The March of the Wooden Soldiers. Except he'd be too short!

Nick glanced quickly through the rest of the pictures while sipping his ice tea and decided that they were innocuous testaments to the broad spectrum of personalities residing at Marsden Grove, with only a hint of the crazy fringe element. They would be good publicity for the next quarterly newsletter. He put the pictures back in the envelope and made a mental note to return them to Jane with his thanks. Christina soon called that lunch was ready.

The turmoil of the morning meeting, the stifling heat of the day and a glass of wine at lunch, all contributed to making Nick feel tired in mid-afternoon. It was not his habit, but he decided to take a nap.

While Christina read quietly downstairs and Charley snoozed on his cushion by her side, Nick retreated upstairs, drew the blinds and, without undressing except for removing his shoes, lay on the bed above the covers. The audible hum of the central air conditioning unit, running continuously to keep the townhouse cool, was a soothing white noise.

As groggy as he felt, he could not fall asleep. He was in a strange state of semi-wakefulness where his eyes were closed but his brain was actively pursuing some undefined object on a sub-conscious circuit before pushing the object up to the fully conscious level. He half dozed in this twilight state until his brain snapped to attention and he bolted upright from the bed.

There was something in those pictures, some little detail his eyes had seen and sent the image to the brain; the brain had stored it but then kept trying to tie it together with other thoughts currently bumping around in his head about the murder until, PRESTO, a slight connection was achieved.

Without retrieving his shoes, he rushed downstairs, startling Christina and the snoozing Charley with his electric movements. He rushed into the small adjacent room where his desk was and extracted a magnifying glass from the top drawer. Returning to the family room and, ignoring Charley's greetings and Christina's quizzical looks, he grabbed the envelope from the coffee table and, without bothering to sit down, flipped through the pictures until he found the right one.

He studied the picture carefully. There was no mistaking it. It was there! This could be a possible link to the past. Granted, it was a long shot but he just had a feeling about this. But how should he pursue it? It wasn't something he could call Jonathan about because it was too flimsy, too nebulous. Besides, Jonathan was away for the weekend, celebrating his grandson's birthday with his family. He decided on the spot that it was worth a risk; he would gamble and face it head-on. He had to know! NOW!

He rushed upstairs and slipped into his shoes and put the one picture that had triggered this excited speculation into his pants pocket. Hurrying downstairs, he called to a bewildered Christina, "Honey, I have to see a resident. Be back shortly," before rushing out the door. Only then did it dawn on him. He **hoped** he'd be back soon. He could be rushing headlong into danger. Yet, considering all the circumstances, something told him that the danger was not grave. He was functioning purely on gut instinct. Still, waves of apprehension overtook him as he reached his destination and knocked on the door.

28

"Hope this isn't a bad time but could I see you for a minute?" he asked.

Clearly surprised by his appearance on her doorstep, she hesitated as confusion registered in her expression. Nick thought it was understandable since they had never been social. Then she smiled, opened the door wider and invited him in.

"I was just making some fresh lemonade," she said softly. "It's such a hot day, we have to drink lots of liquids. Would you like some?"

"Great!" he said as she led him into the family room. Her townhouse had the same layout as his. On the mantel over the gas fireplace he spotted a series of old family pictures, with that sepia tint that infuses photographs of by-gone eras. They depicted in various poses a family: mother, father and three small girls, seemingly close in age. Two pictures showed the family on a sailboat."

"Your family?" he asked.

She looked up from where she was pouring the lemonade and, as she glanced at him where he was standing next to the mantel, her entire expression momentarily changed and she was stunningly somber. Her eyes clouded over. The next second she gave him a shy smile and nodded yes.

Nick studied the three happy children in their various poses with their equally happy parents— the universal prototype of a well-fed, healthy, contented, flourishing family unit. He tried to distinguish which child might be she but they all looked alike with their overall blondness, crisp features and sturdy bodies.

"Which one is you?" he asked as she moved toward him with two tall glasses of ice-chilled lemonade.

"I'm usually the one with the goofiest grin," she said, not looking at the row of pictures.

"Did you enjoy sailing?" he asked, pointing to one of the pictures of the family on a sailboat, while thinking of the seaman's knot used to hang Emma Craig.

"Very much," she said, still not looking toward the mantel's pictures. "It was our family's major outlet when my father wasn't working."

She handed him his lemonade and they sat in two comfortable chairs flanking the fireplace, facing each other. She took a long sip of her drink, then looked at him expectantly. He collected his thoughts before deciding on his approach.

"This is awkward," he said as an opening remark with a half-smile, "but I saw something in the picture that Jane took of you this morning that aroused my curiosity."

She stared at him with a fixed expression that was inscrutable. Was it one of interest, earnestness, hostility, perplexity or defensiveness? He couldn't decide. He continued.

"You were waving at the camera and your arm was raised and the sleeve of your blouse had fallen back, exposing your arm."

She sat silent and immobile, like a statue, her enigmatic expression never changing, her body frozen in time and space.

"And unless I'm very much mistaken, I saw a tattoo on the underside of your arm, a tattoo of numbers. I studied these under a magnifying glass and I believe them to be from a concentration camp."

Nick withdrew the picture from his pants pocket and thrust it toward her. "It is a concentration camp number, isn't it, Helen?" he said, like some clever lawyer coaxing a confession. "I wondered why you always wore long-sleeve tops for your strenuous workouts, even on the hottest days. Now I understand."

Her gaze shifted to the proffered photo but she made no motion to take it. All she finally said was a soft "Yes."

Nick felt like he was balancing on a high wire at dizzying heights, taking each step cautiously, not sure what the next step might bring or even sure where this was all leading to, but he pressed on.

"I know this was the worst experience any human being could possibly have and I don't mean to pry, but I've known a few people who, like you, were concentration camp survivors and they wore their numbers proudly. You must have overcome so much to arrive here at Marsden Grove at this stage of life. Your story, I'm sure, is an inspiring tale of surmounting overwhelming challenges and not only surviving but prospering. Your number should be a badge of honor for the triumph it represents."

Nick halted, not sure what to say next or where this was leading to. Fortunately, Helen now took the lead.

"Excuse me for a minute," was all she said, casually. As she headed for the downstairs bathroom, she added, "Please pour us some more lemonade."

By the time Nick had poured the lemonade and placed the glasses on the small table between their two chairs, Helen was back, and they again took their seats. She no longer had a far-away look in her eyes; now she looked focused and relaxed, as she gazed directly at him and began to speak.

'It was clever of you to observe such a small detail from the photo. Yes, I am a concentration camp survivor, but, no, unlike those other survivors you refer to, I don't wear my number as a badge of honor."

Helen paused to take a sip of lemonade and continued.

"You see, Nick, I didn't triumph over the horrors I experienced during the war. The war made me into a monster of hate and I've dedicated my life to seeking revenge. Many Americans probably think that only the Jews were victims of the Nazi atrocity machine. My family was not Jewish. My parents were communists, and we lived in a small village. After the Germans invaded Poland, we were packed off to a concentration camp—my mother, father, two sisters and I. We were moved several times and finally taken to Auschwitz. My father was in a different section of the camp and we learned of his death soon after our arrival. He had been shot, but for what reason, we never learned.

"My mother was on a work detail and wasted away in front of our eyes, sharing her meager food portion with my two sisters, Amelie and Bronka, and me. My real name is Halinka."

Helen's gaze shifted away from Nick and her voice took a lower pitch, more steely in tone, as though she were reliving long-past experiences.

"At Auschwitz there was a Dr. Mueller, who assisted Dr. Horst Schumann in performing sterilization experiments on young girls, mostly Jews but some Poles. Amelie was fifteen and Bronka was thirteen when he started his work on them. I was twelve and didn't understand what he was doing but I saw their horrible suffering before they both died. Dr. Mueller was also a sexual sadist who selected me as his personal outlet for beatings and rapes. When he tired of me, I was only fourteen and he had me transported to a special brothel for servicing German soldiers. In the last confusing days of the war, as the German order collapsed, I and two other girls escaped from the brothel and made our way to the advancing American line."

Helen abruptly stopped and Nick, overwhelmed by her story, was speechless. A long silence followed. Finally, Helen shifted in her chair and fixed Nick with a look of glaring intensity.

"I was fifteen when the war ended. My village, I discovered, was gone and so were all my relations. I was a used, broken body with a broken spirit to match. I could never have children. I thought of suicide constantly but there was one spark left in me and that was a spark of hate. Unlimited hate! The monsters had made me a monster, good for nothing except hate and revenge. At fifteen, I vowed that I would get my revenge on Dr. Mueller, but not just on him. If it took me the rest of my life, I would wipe out his entire family as he had wiped out mine. That's what I dedicated my life to; that's what kept me going; that's what made me strong.

"I learned that he had somehow escaped prosecution as a war criminal and I spent years searching for him, finally discovering that he had come to America with his wife and two children and had changed his name to Strelitz."

Helen's voice changed in tone but Nick noticed that her speech was now slightly slurred.

"I followed him to New York, called him up and told him I was reporting him to the authorities and the next night he committed suicide. Several months earlier his wife had died of cancer. What the hospital records never showed was that her life support system was disconnected—not by a hospital official at the request of the family but by me, late at night, while the duty nurse dozed. That gave me satisfaction but the daughters were still my ultimate targets. It took me decades but I was relentless. I spent years working as a hotel maid while I earned a degree in accounting. As soon as I had some financial security I returned to my life's mission: revenge for my family. The older sister had changed her name again from Strelitz to Steele and eventually, after many years, I finally tracked her down in Pennsylvania. Then I found Emma, living under her married name, here in Marsden Grove. I had to make the sister's death in Pennsylvania look like an unplanned hit-and-run so I could be free to pursue the other sister."

Nick was observing Helen's features appearing to lose all tautness and her speech was definitely slowing down. She now gave him a half-smile.

"I thought the ultimate victory for my revenge would be to go unpunished for the two daughters' deaths so I tried to disguise my vengeance. Still, I wanted them to know that I knew their father's history and that they must pay, too. I had given that parrot to Emma with its reference to sins because I knew it would torment her. You almost caught me when I had to kill the bird because it saw me enter Emma's home and kill her and went crazy when it saw me again that morning. I just managed to get far enough away from the pool area to appear as if I was out on a jog and returning to the gym."

"How did you gain entry into Emma's home?" Nick had to ask.

"I knew Gillie had a drinking problem, so I left a good bottle of whiskey on his desk. Remember, the gym and his office are close by and each has an entrance through the recreation room. After a mid-afternoon workout, I wandered over to his office and saw that he had consumed a lot of the whiskey and was asleep at his desk. His key ring was attached to his belt with an elasticized cord, so I found the key to his locked desk drawer and took the master kay to all the units. Two days later, after I had killed Emma, I put it on the floor by his desk when he was out on a job."

"And Rosemary?"

"She was the last of the line and had to go. She put up a great struggle but all my strength building exercises helped me overcome her. I wanted to get everything over with before I lost either my physical ability or my mental processes. I would have been eighty-five this coming October."

Nick noted Helen's use of the future perfect tense. Helen's breathing was suddenly becoming labored. Her eyes were half- closed.

""You don't have to worry, Nick," she said with a pause before each word and a slight rueful smile. "I'm not a danger to anyone else. I've accomplished what I set out to do and it's time for me to depart. You'll find a written history of everything I told you in the Bible on my night stand. Do you know, Nick, that in the entire Bible, both Old and New Testaments, you can't find one passage that condones vengeance. Vengeance is strictly God's jurisdiction. I've never found any justification for what I dedicated my life to doing, except for the faces of my mother and two sisters that have haunted me forever. And one more face: the face of Dr. Mueller when he would beat and torture and rape and debase me. I had to establish my own set of rules to deal with those images and that's what I did."

Her body suddenly slumped forward as the lemonade glass crashed to the floor. Nick rushed to her side and rested her head against the back of her chair. Her words were merely whispers.

"I've taken the necessary pills to get me out of here fast. There's nothing you can do, so please don't bother."

Nick thought about calling 911 but hesitated as a titanic ethical battle waged within him. Did he have a moral obligation to try to preserve Helen's life, against her wishes and in the face of the criminal charges she would surely face? Had the soul of this woman been so warped by the horrendous tortures she endured as a child, that despite the revenge she had wreaked upon three innocent women of a monster forebear, which no moral code could justify, was allowing her to die the humane way of balancing the scales? He knew he was neither a religious man nor a deep moral thinker, and certainly, in a situation like this, he couldn't call up some abstract philosophical principles to be an indisputable guide. All he could do was follow his gut instinct, as he had been doing all afternoon.

Helen's eyes were now shut. Her breathing came in short, shallow gasps, her body lay limply against the deep cushions of her wingback chair, her head slumped against one corner.

Nick went upstairs, found the Bible and the neatly handwritten and signed confession. Suddenly, the implication of his role in Helen's suicide hit him. He wiped his fingerprints off the Bible and the paper and left it where he had found it.

When he returned downstairs Helen had stopped breathing. He checked her pulse and found none. He dialed 911. "I want to report a death," he said and gave Helen's name and address. He sat quietly and plotted the few minor changes in the story he would give to the police. The EMTs arrived in under three minutes along with the police and they worked on Helen to no avail. He answered all the questions posed by the police and was told he was free to go.

He walked slowly toward his townhouse, a dazed man, pondering all the implications of the tragic unfolding history he had just heard. He knew that Helen's story would haunt him forever, as he recycled questions of evil and justice and moral depravity and spiritual death. He had been given a glimpse of what Joseph Conrad called "the heart of darkness," and he would never be the same.

Christina took one look at Nick when he walked through the front door and exclaimed "What happened to you? You look like you've just come back from a war!"

In one sense, Nick thought, it had been a war, but it was a battle waged within himself and no one was declared a winner. He slumped into his favorite leather chair, suddenly feeling dead tired. Christina sat on the arm of his chair, saying nothing, just stroking his hair gently while Charley, with equal empathy, silently nuzzled his face against Nick's hip, his large black eyes gazing expressively up at his master

Nick felt love and solicitude surrounding him and thought of Helen's loss of parents and sisters by the age of thirteen and her degradation and abuse by monsters for the next two years. He vividly recalled her comment about never being able to have children, so from thirteen to eighty-four she had been alone, left adrift all those years with nothing to build upon, only the secrets of her broken past to avenge. Impulsively, he pulled

Christina down onto his lap, hugging her fiercely, and buried his head in her shoulder as he felt himself crying, in gratitude for what he had and in shame for what humans were capable of doing to one another.

29

Word of the EMT van and the police car followed by the cordoning off of Helen's townhouse spread rapidly across the community and Nick's phone never stopped ringing. For the first time he abdicated his responsibility at the urging of Christina.

"You've had enough!" she said decisively. "We're getting out of here." She quickly got Charley's leash and led both dog and man out the front door to her car. As they drove away, Nick glanced at the rear-view mirror on the passenger's side and saw the Major, Big Foot and Cat Lady marching toward his receding townhouse. Let them handle things for a change, and I don't care if they screw everything up, he thought, jubilant to be escaping.

Christina stopped at an Indian restaurant in her town and ordered takeout which they ate on her deck while watching a beautiful sunset.

Early the next morning they took Charley for a long walk along the beach. Charley loved his romps in the Preserve next to Marsden Grove, but he was in dog heaven at the beach. Nick found a discarded Frisbee and kept tossing it into the roiling waters, to Charley's sheer delight. He'd rush fearlessly into the surf and paddle out to the bobbing Frisbee and dutifully bring it back to Nick, then shake himself free of excess water, as Christina dodged the spraying deluge and Nick laughed at both their antics.

Upon returning to Christina's house, her phone was ringing. It was Jonathan.

"Nick, the news of Helen's suicide reached me last night in Pennsylvania so I came back early. The officer who questioned you had some doubts about a few of your answers."

"Did they find Helen's written confession?" Nick asked.

"What confession?"

"Helen's written and signed confession that she killed Emma, Emma's sister in Pennsylvania and Rosemary. "

A long, shrill whistle came from Jonathan's end of the line.

"I'll explain everything, but I don't want to go back to Marsden Grove and face all the crazies just now. Can you come here to Christina's house? We'll have breakfast and I'll give you all the details. You won't believe your ears."

"Put the coffee on," Jonathan said. Nick gave him the address and he was at the door in less than twenty minutes.

Nick felt complete trust in Jonathan and, over a hearty breakfast, told him everything exactly the way it happened, including his indecision about making some last-minute attempt to prevent Helen's suicide but, after listening to her history and reading her confession, deciding to let her go.

Jonathan listened with his quiet attentiveness even as he consumed another waffle and had more coffee. When Nick finished his story, he looked directly at Jonathan and asked, "Did I fuck up or did I do the right thing?"

Jonathan swallowed his last bit of sausage, drained his coffee mug, wiped his mouth and placed his napkin on the table before answering. "I've learned in my business that things aren't always black or white, right or wrong. Is a wife who kills her husband after years of his physically abusing her and the children, guilty of murder when she's finally taken enough and snaps? The law says Helen was guilty of three premeditated murders, but from what you tell me she and her family suffered at the hands of the Nazis, who knows if her mind was ever capable of making sane, objective decisions when it came to the man who destroyed her and her sisters.

"I'm not a psychiatrist and I'm not a judge and I'm not a jury. And I'm certainly not God. But in a sense I play God, judge and jury when I'm confronted with ambiguous circumstances and I have to make a judgment call. I look at the facts of this case and I see a young girl surviving unimaginable torments and abuse that, it seems to me, would be enough to warp anybody for life. Helen suffered enough! In your shoes, I would have done the same thing."

Jonathan smiled. "I'll take care of the details. You've got nothing to worry about. This case is closed."

Relief flooded Nick's face, not just for no longer having to worry about being implicated in Helen's suicide, but for the strong support Jonathan was giving him. As they sat at Christina's table, drinking more coffee and chatting randomly about other topics, Nick knew with certainty that he had made a friend for life.

30

Life quickly returned to near-normal at Marsden Grove now that the murders of Emma Craig and her daughter had been solved.

The local papers were filled with the details of a family vendetta, dating back to atrocities committed during WW II, relieving many residents who had been convinced of a serial killer on the loose. Still, some of the more excitable souls clung to the belief that crime was on the rise everywhere, the younger generation was out of control, and they were going to keep a gun (at least a toy pistol taken from a grandson) or a kitchen knife or Mace or a baseball bat or a knitting needle or a rolling pin by their bed, just in case. One resident happily discovered a dual advantage to her bedpan: for use in an emergency and as a heavy, blunt, defensive instrument.

The week after the papers had exhausted every angle of Emma's death and Helen's suicide, Fran Walker returned. She simply said that her sister had miraculously recovered and gave no further details. Residents took note, however, of a light tan Fran was sporting that no amount of pale makeup could conceal.

Vera Parks was still unable to sell her unit because of the ridiculous price she was asking. The battling Moriaritys were still battling and the Clarks were still drinking, according to those who keenly observed the frequency of liquor deliveries being made to their townhouse, and Henry Cushman was still shacking up with Violet Tomby but now they were doing it openly. Dagmar Neilson was still on her "save the environment" crusade.

When the election for the Board of Managers was over, Sonia Arcadivich was the surprising winner, beating Dagmar Neilson and the Major. The Major had insisted on a recount but that verified Sonia's victory.

"Great!" Nick exclaimed. "Now we'll have government by the stars and the Ouija board!" That was the final straw. Nick resigned from the Board, put his townhouse up for sale at a price consistent with current market values, and was in contract within two weeks.

One night in mid-September, Nick was jarred from sleep by sirens and a voice coming through a bullhorn directing people to leave their homes immediately as a gas leak had been reported—the entire community was fueled by natural gas--and an explosion could occur at any moment.

Nick threw his bathrobe over his pajamas, hurried downstairs, grabbed Charley's leash and quickly leashed the excited dog as they flew out of the house. General panic ensued as residents rushed out of their homes in the middle of the night and more of Marsden Grove's secrets were suddenly revealed.

Celeste Grayson, the refined Hamptons' matron appeared in full dominatrix regalia—black leather from head to stiletto-heeled boots—everything but a whip, with the young woman who shared her home in a white Greek slave tunic. Also exiting Celeste's home with her was Jack Skelly, the pornography collector and George Trumble, looking ridiculous in a sheer black nightie revealing a black thong. Never had the garments of Victoria's Secret looked more un-alluring than on George's hairy, pudgy body. Evidently, this foursome had formed a little play group of their own.

Even George Perkins, Nick's golf buddy and playboy, made an unexpected appearance that night, rushing from the townhouse of Mabel Thomas, the community flirt. The town stud and the playgirl of the senior set had finally found each other, if only momentarily.

Jane Curtis, the Cat Lady, finally showed that she possessed five cats and not two as the by-laws allowed. She stood on the street, clutching two in each arm while the fifth cat perched precariously on her shoulder.

Jessie Knowles, aka Big Foot, lumbered forth from his townhouse dressed in a voluminous nightshirt of red and white stripes that made him look like Big Rock Candy Mountain.

The Major was one of the last residents to appear, draped only in a towel since he had obviously been taking a shower. Most of his scrawny body and all his patriotic tattoos were clearly on display. Jack Moriarity, ever the jokester, when he wasn't battling with his wife, snuck up behind him and pulled his towel off. Taken totally by surprise, the Major froze and then doubled over in modesty. But not before several eyes had scrutinized and appraised his private parts. From that night forward, he was comically referred to as Major Minor.

The origin of the gas leak was discovered and corrected and residents were allowed to return to their homes. But enough intimate secrets had been revealed to keep the community buzzing for weeks.

31

They decided on a beach wedding in late September. Nick was overjoyed when Christina told him shortly after the day that Jonathan had come to her home for breakfast that she had changed her mind and was ready for a full commitment with him.

When Nick asked her what made her change her mind, she unhesitatingly replied, "It was the empathy you showed for Helen."

Tom was his father's best man, and, of course, Charley was the proud and properly behaved ring bearer. Christina's son Garth flew in from Italy the week before the ceremony and did not seem pleased to see his mother's starting a new life with a man he didn't know. He and Nick went out to dinner one night alone, at Christina's urging, but, still, it didn't seem to soften Garth's edge. He had made some cutting remarks at dinner the night before the wedding and Christina had quietly but firmly told him that if he could not accept her marriage to Nick, then he could not be a part of her life. That seemed to have a sobering effect on Garth who was noticeably more pleasant the next day.

"It will take time but he'll come around, I'm sure," Christina had told Nick, who was impressed with the strong ultimatum she had given her son. "He's an adult and we will mostly lead separate lives, but we'll always be family as long as he behaves properly towards us, because you're number one in my life now." she said with finality. Nick could sense the steely fiber behind her resolution, and the love and commitment her attitude conveyed.

Among the few dozen guests were Jonathan and his lady friend, Mary Lou. After the brief beach ceremony performed by a friend of Christina's who was a Universalist minister, the casual reception was held on the deck of Christina's home where another canine guest made his appearance. His name was Baxter and he had been Rosemary Craig's dog, whose barking drew the attention of Rosemary's neighbor who discovered the body. A golden lab of sweet disposition, when no one was claiming him after Rosemary's death, Jonathan took him.

Prior to Nick's wedding day, Jonathan had brought Baxter over to Nick's townhouse to meet Charley and it was brotherly bonding at first sight. Nick and Jonathan had taken the two dogs for a long tramp through the Preserve. Although both approaching middle age in dog years, they leaped and frolicked, barked and scavenged, raced and wrestled, exulting in their comradeship like young pups, until they wore themselves out. Upon returning to Nick's townhouse, they both drank from Charley's water bowl and then, with no hesitation, curled themselves side by side, one brown, one yellow, on Charley's oversized dog cushion.

"Why am I suddenly reminded of what Rick says as the closing line in *Casablanca*?" Nick asked Jonathan, gazing at the two dogs, their eyes already closed. Both men said the line together while laughing, "Louis, I think this is the beginning of a beautiful relationship."

The guests were departing after several hours of post-nuptial celebrations, but Nick had asked Jonathan and Mary Lou to stay. Both Nick and Christina had taken an instant shine to Mary Lou and wanted to know her better. When the four of them were finally alone, Christina and Nick excused themselves to change into beach clothes. When they returned from the bedroom, they found Mary Lou and Jonathan cleaning up.

"Don't do that!" Nick said.

"Let's just get the food wrapped and into the refrigerator so it doesn't spoil," Mary Lou sensibly suggested.

Now it was Christina's turn at directing traffic. "Nick, why don't you and Jonathan get a fire going in our fire pit down on the beach and we'll join you as soon as we get the food put away. We should have a great sunset tonight."

"Sounds like a plan," Nick said.

With Charley and Baxter happily dogging their footsteps, Nick and Jonathan toted four folding chairs and several pieces of cut driftwood down the wooden stairway leading to the beach. Nick remembered to bring four glasses and an uncorked bottle of champagne to toast the sunset.

Both dogs hoped for a long, exploratory romp along the beach but saw their masters busily constructing a fire in a dug-out hole in the sand, so they contented themselves with chasing each other in and out of the water.

Having finished their chores, the two men sat on the folding chairs side by side, facing the oncoming sunset, the two dogs now settling by their sides.

"It looks like you're sailing into a sunny future, Nick. Congratulations."

Nick smiled broadly. "I feel like a very lucky man to have known love with two extraordinary woman like my Judy and now Christina."

"Will you move here permanently when you close on your townhouse in Marsden Grove?"

"We've talked about that. Christina loves this place and I do, too, but it's a little cramped for the two of us full-time. We've already discussed plans to nearly double the space by adding a second story. She's excited about that and so am I."

"That's a good idea, but it can be really messy," Jonathan said. "And it usually takes twice the time the contractor quoted you." He paused, then said, "I've got a condo on the North Fork, in Calverton. Two bedrooms, two baths and a nice water view. I've had it for years and use it as a rental property. The lease on my current renter is ending in two months, so if you want to proceed with the renovations to this place and need a temporary home, consider it yours."

"That's thoughtful, Jonathan. What's the rent?"

"Who's talking about rent? The place is yours for as long as you need it, no charge."

"That's really kind, but we couldn't deprive you of an income stream," Nick protested.

Jonathan's voice took on that steely edge that Nick had heard before. "I consider you a friend and friends do favors for friends without making a profit."

"I'll discuss it with Christina and get back to you. This is just the goose we need to finalize plans for this house. Thanks."

The two men fell into a sustained silence which, Nick reflected, felt comfortable. Finally, Jonathan said, "I never really thanked you, Nick, for breaking the case. Nobody is giving you the credit but you solved the mystery of the deaths of both Emma and Rosemary."

"I just happened to hit on the right detail and followed that up," Nick said.

"But if you hadn't spotted Helen's concentration camp tattoo in that photo, we could still be whistling in the dark, so don't dismiss what you did. It could have been a damn fool thing to confront Helen if her focus wasn't on that family exclusively, but you treated her humanely once you heard the whole story and let her go out the way she wanted."

Nick was both pleased and slightly embarrassed by Jonathan's praise, so he made light of it. "Am I supposed to say, 'Awh, shucks!'

and kick the sand now?" he said in a mock hillbilly drawl.

Jonathan smiled, dug into his pants pocket and produced a rolled up piece of parchment paper. Without looking directly at Nick, he handed the paper to him. Nick unrolled it and saw what looked like an official document, complete with calligraphic writing, signature lines and a seal. Once his eyes focused on the details, a broad smile swept across his face.

"I got it on ebay," Jonathan explained as Nick read.

Nick Dalton had been made a Junior Detective, First-Class, in the Dick Tracy Fan Club. Next to the signature of Dick Tracy, Nick saw that of Jonathan Grimes.

"For Christmas I want my two-way radio wrist watch," Nick exclaimed.

As Christina and Mary Lou descended the stairs to the beach, they saw the two men, sitting in their folding chairs but leaning towards each other, and, like two kids plotting some grand high jinks, roaring with laughter. Echoing their masters' joy, with their long, feathery tails whipping up sprays of sand in all directions, both Charley and Baxter were barking deliriously.

The sunset that evening, everyone agreed, was glorious.

Mys Bat   8/20/18

✓

CIRC 2019 ✓ ✓

CPSIA information can be obtained at www.ICGtesting.com
Printed in the USA
BVOW07s1956250914
367964BV00002B/5/P

9 781600 479885